Malibu Angel

By
Mia Fox

Published by Evatopia Press
www.evatopia.com

ISBN: 978-1-63099-057-2

Cover Design by Evatopia Inc.

Interior book design by
Bob Houston eBook Formatting

Acknowledgements

I would like to give credit and sincere thanks to Victoria Zumbrum who asked me if I could write a story about a guardian angel. I hope I've met your expectations. I truly appreciate the inspiration. I never imagined that it would give way to an entire new series.

Many thanks to the eagle eyes of Jessica Molina Ramirez and Ginelle Blanch for catching my errors...or is it the error of my ways?! You're both wonderful friends.

Thank you to Bob Houston who formats all of my books and never complains when a week later he is asked to add "just one little thing."

Evatopia Press for coordinating cover art and marketing.

Most importantly, to my family...I love you so much. Thank you for sending me to my room...to write!

Prologue

"Diane! Your caramel macchiato is on the bar. Double foam latte with an extra shot of espresso for Layla!"

As the barista called out orders, loyal customers shuffled bleary-eyed to the front of the line, anticipating their first caffeine jolt of the day. While most waited in sleepy silence, one woman drew everyone's attention. Her cherubic face was accented by dimples and framed in golden curls; her green eyes shone brightly in spite of the early hour. But aside from her natural beauty, she was recognized because Angeline was as forgetful as she was kind, and as clumsy as she was pretty.

"Mornin' Angeline, can I start your white mocha with coconut milk? One or two?"

"Two," she confirmed. "Thanks, Tom. That'd be great," she called from her place in line. "Plus a cinnamon scone for my friend outside," she said referring to the homeless man parked by the entrance.

"You got it."

"I don't know how Tom remembers everyone's orders...let alone their names. Imagine me doing this job," Angeline commented to her friend, but before getting an answer, her phone's ring chimed at her. She looked at it in horror.

"Just pretend the call dropped." Her friend instantly knew what caused a frown to cross Angeline's pretty features as she had first-hand experience with waiting on hold and promptly being forgotten.

Angeline smiled and gave the thumb's up signal as she answered the call. "Hi. I don't know what happened. The call must've dropped. So...can you give me that tracking number again? 2-3-6-X-T-What? Can you repeat that?" Angeline pressed her cell phone closer to her ear, then tapped the shoulder of her friend standing in front her. "Do you have a pen?" she whispered, covering the phone's mouthpiece. Her friend produced a pen from her purse and handed it over.

With her hands full, Angeline gave a momentary look of helplessness. Finally, she opened her mouth adorably, indicating her friend should place the pen between her teeth to which her friend delivered a no-way-you've-got-to-be-kidding look. "Okay, can you hold this?" asked Angeline, handing over a hefty pile of papers to her friend before she could protest.

"Yep, I'm here, Mr. Walker. Sorry, the connection is really bad and it's super noisy here." She shook the pen and tried scribbling on the scratch paper tucked into her hand to no avail. She turned to a heavy-set man behind her. "Do you mind if I write on your back? I can't get it to work without a firm surface," she explained indicating the pen. Upon receiving attention from Angeline, the man immediately froze with nerves and began to sweat.

Undeterred, Angeline smiled angelically and motioned for him to turn around. But when he did, his considerable girth bumped into a deliciously handsome man who had been listening and watching her with amusement.

"Here, try this one," he offered, handing another pen around the mid-section of the man standing between their potentially blooming love affair. Their hands met; their eyes sparked with intention.

"Thanks, that's really kind of you," Angeline beamed.

"Any time. I'm…"

"Yes, Mr. Walker, I'm here. What else can I do for you?" Angeline shrugged her shoulders at the man in apology and her call continued.

Unable to continue his introduction, let alone the momentary distraction brought on by Angeline, the handsome man returned to his place in line. That place was disappointingly one person too far away from where she stood.

Her boss' voice brought her back to less pleasant thoughts than the man who still wore a smile after his brief encounter with her. "Mr. Walker! I don't think that's part of my job description. Yes, I appreciate that you think I'm hotter than a latte, but really! Yes, I'll be there soon...although I've got a mind not to come in at all."

She hung up and turned to her friend. "Did you hear that?"

"Me and everyone else," she said, motioning to an elderly woman three places ahead in line. The woman nodded sweetly, but then turned back to face the front.

Angeline pulled at her hair in frustration. "I can't help but get a little worked up. This is my third job in three months. I think I'm going to have to tell the employment agency no more male bosses." Then, remembering something important, she suddenly opened her mouth and covered it with her hand. "Oh, I told the guy handling my account that I was leaving his agency."

"He hit on you?"

Angeline nodded. "You know, it's funny. A year ago I would never have had the guts to leave so many jobs without having one to fall back on, but now..." she shook her head as if to validate that she couldn't be compromised. "Now, I see...signs. That's the only way to describe it," she said emphatically. "Signs that tell me I haven't met the right guy, but he's out there. I feel it. And, I shouldn't have to put up with bosses who have more interest in...you know...than my mind."

"So are you seeing 'signs' that you should quit your job...again?"

Angeline stood a bit straighter and tilted her head upwards, appearing as if she were sniffing the air, much like a dog anticipating the return of his owner or the presence of danger. "Not yet...," she admitted, tapping the pen against her chin absentmindedly.

Keeping her voice low, she spoke to her friend. "Oh, I nearly forgot that I still have the hottie's pen."

Turning once again to the rotund guy behind her, she asked, "Can you pass this back?" She indicated the man who stood behind him, and smiled as he blew a kiss at her. She responded by pretending to catch it mid-air.

As if to interrupt their flirtation, her phone rang on cue and she promptly looked at the screen. "Boss man, again," she said to her friend.

"Hello Mr. Walker, I'm still waiting in line. It's a bit of a crawl."

She paused to listen to his response and then her mouth opened wide along with her eyes showing both horror and shock. "Mr. Walker! How dare you! I have self-respect, which means no job is worth listening to you ask me to crawl on all fours imitating a horny cat on a hot tin roof. I never! And, I quit. You'll have to get your own mocha today."

She hung up the phone with a flourish and shook her head to herself while a few customers waiting for drinks craned their neck to stare at Angeline with a mixture of shock and amusement to which she simply smiled and explained, "My boss is sort of a lecherous ass. One of the reasons I'm trying to start my own business."

She indicated the pile of papers and notebooks in her arms as well as those being held by her friend. "That was my sign. I guess there's no time like the present." She tapped the guy in front of her as well as the woman in front of him. "Hey, would you all like to see? Feel free to pass this down the line. It's better than just waiting." She was just starting to pass around a portfolio containing her new bikini designs when her phone rang once again.

"He must really be in need of his coffee this morning," she said to anyone willing to listen including the handsome man who was still painfully just out of reach.

"Oh, you're not my boss," she answered with a decidedly happier tone. "My brochures? You can have them done early? Yes! Oh thank you. Let me grab a pen..."

Without waiting to be asked, the pen made its way up the line and back to her again.

"Honestly, Angeline, I'm not going to be able to show my face in here again." Her friend watched the shenanigans going back and forth, and shook her head in embarrassment.

"It's nothing, Britlyn. These are my peeps. My future customers."

"Even that guy?" Britlyn motioned with her chin to the big guy behind Angeline.

"Could be. He might have a girlfriend."

Her friend got a glint in her eye and leaned in closer. "Maybe you should find out if the cutie behind him has a girlfriend."

Angeline used the big guy as a shield and peered behind him to catch another glimpse. No sooner spotted, she jumped back and realized her call was still on hold. "Oh shoot! Yes, I'm back. Can I get that confirmation number?" She balanced the phone in the crook of her neck while rummaging in her purse for another piece of paper and trying not to drop the two notebooks that she was carrying. No use.

As the line moved forward and Angeline tried to keep up, one of the books fell from under her arm and as she tried to catch it, the other slipped as well. In trying to maneuver quickly she only managed to slip on a tile where someone spilled a drop of coffee. In spite of it being a small area, the wet floor was her enemy.

She stumbled backwards, appearing as if she would land right on her butt, but conveniently fell into the arms of the chubby guy in line behind her. He seemed as surprised as Angeline to find her lodged in his arms.

"Are you okay?" The handsome man didn't waste a minute to inquire about her well-being. Stepping out of his place in line, he moved in front of the overweight man that had a firm grasp on Angeline, who appeared to be a rag doll in his beefy arms.

Looking up at the man standing before her, she beamed. "Yeah, I'm fine. It's all good."

"It's nothing new for Grace here," chimed her friend, Britlyn.

Angeline sent her a half-hearted smirk before attempting to get on her feet. The gorgeous man tapped the overweight guy on the shoulder. "Hey buddy, you can let her go now."

As if only then realizing that he was still holding her by the arms, the guy pulled

Angeline up to a standing position and released her.

"Well, thanks!" Angeline's bubbly voice charmed both men who stared as if hoping for more time with her, but fate stepped in.

"Angel? You gonna pick up these drinks?" The barista called out. "Or are we going to see another floor show?"

"On my way," she said, reaching for one of those handy cardboard trays.

"No way," the barista said. "I'll get them." He removed the drinks from her hands, which she was attempting rather unsuccessfully to shove into their cardboard spots. With a simple twist the barista lodged both drinks in place and handed the tray over. "You have a safe day, you hear?"

The two women headed outdoors with much fanfare as Angeline balanced her tray along with her paperwork. "How embarrassing was that?"

Britlyn smiled, but gave her a look as if to say that this was nothing new. "Not only are you clumsy, but you've got bad timing."

"What do you mean?"

"Well, if you had arrived just moments later, you could have been standing in front of that gorgeous guy and then you would have landed in his arms. I guess your guardian angel isn't doing his job."

# # #

Chapter One

"Sam, did you hear that?"

An angel wearing a smirk that was decidedly more devilish than his title, faced his judge. "It's not true," he said with a shake of his head, golden waves of his hair blowing slightly with the breeze. "She wasn't the least bit harmed. Not even a twisted ankle. That guy caught her in one swift motion."

"Did he?"

"Yeah, you saw him. If he hadn't been there, she probably would have fallen on her beautiful behin..."

"Never mind! Or, the other guy would have caught her. You know, *The One*. That handsome fella who was actually supposed to be behind her in line."

Sam's clear, blue eyes flashed with guilt. Caught...again. "I'm...uh. I'm not sure what you mean."

The judge wiggled his eyebrows at Sam. "And the phone calls? Right when that chap was trying to introduce himself? Sam, I must say that was almost bordering on being rude. I'm surprised," he said with a tisk of his tongue and a shake of his head.

Sam swallowed hard. "Perhaps you're remembering the incident differently than I am. I...uh...I was just trying to...to..."

"Shall we take a look at what happened just minutes before the incident?" The judge stared at Sam, daring him to defy the request. "Very well," he continued as a flash of light broke the silence. A screen materialized and a view of the coffee shop was projected onto it.

We see Angeline enter from earlier in the morning and closely behind is the gorgeous guy who gave her his pen. He opens the door for her and she turns to smile. He's just about to follow her inside, when the chubby guy comes barreling through. "Oh, thanks man!" he says and proceeds to enter and stand directly behind beautiful Angeline in line.

The judge claps his hands and the screen vanishes. Sam looks skyward, seeming to wish that another show would begin. Anything to take the attention away from himself.

"Do you have anything to say for yourself?" the judge asks more sternly than Sam would have expected.

"I may have sort of helped that guy...kind of hurried him along. But, I had good intentions in placing him next in line. He's lactose intolerant. I worried that he'd faint if he didn't get food fast."

The judge shakes his head and rolls his eyes. "The condition that requires food frequently is hypoglycemia. It means one's blood sugar drops to low levels. Lactose intolerant means he can't digest dairy products properly. He could have easily waited in line behind that handsome gentleman...but then, we know what would have happened."

Sam swallowed hard, afraid of the direction the conversation had taken. "We do?"

"Yes. Your human, the one you are supposed to serve as guardian angel to, would have fallen into the arms of a different man and love may have ensued."

Sam shook his head rapidly. "Love? Come on. I don't see that happening. I mean, it was just a few minutes in a coffee line. The barista would have called out her order and interrupted any conversation that could have possibly led to love."

"Is that so?"

"Absolutely. Like I said, I didn't hurry chubs along because of her. I was just thinking of him."

The judge nodded, taking in all the information. "So, you're not in love with your human?"

"Her? Nah, of course not."

"You are supposed to serve and protect her at all costs," he replied.

Sam jumps at the opportunity placed in front of him. "I do! You know I'd do anything for Angeline."

"Angeline?"

Sam blushed. If there was any doubt that he had hung himself out to dry earlier, his faux pas solidified it. He was most certainly caught. "I heard her friend call her name once. But just because I know her name, doesn't mean..."

"That you love her?"

He couldn't even look his judge in the eye. With his head bowed, Sam realized the truth.

"Alright, so maybe I do love her. It would have to be an act of God to prevent it. No offense."

"None taken."

"God, I ask you...how could I not love her? She's beautiful...the way she always drops everything, but then laughs it off. How she always remembers the homeless man outside and brings him a muffin or scone, her face, those eyes, that milky white complexion..."

"You've certainly studied her," the judge noted sternly.

"There's so much more to her than just external beauty. She is kind and brave, smart and witty. I love her with all my being." He pressed his lips into a thin line and shook his head, unable to accept his own imperfection. "I'm sorry."

A kind arm reaches around Sam's shoulders. He is pulled into a warm embrace and visibly calms. "What do I do?" he finally asks.

"You are her guardian angel. That means you protect her from harm, but you must let her life unfold. Doesn't she deserve to find a mate?"

Sam seems to ponder the question. In fact, he ponders it a bit too long.

"Sam?" the judge asks impatiently.

"Yes. Yes, she deserves every happiness...," in a small whisper he adds, "I just wish I were the one to make her happy."

"I'm sorry, Sam. For now, you are here...and she is there. Maybe when your term is served, you will find each other. But when that day comes and you return to Earth once again human, you will not have any memory of your angel assignment, nor Angeline. If the two of you are meant to be, then it shall be so. But for now, you must uphold the laws of the guardian angels."

Sam looks pensive. "I protect her to the best of my abilities." With a heavy heart, he adds, "and I allow life to unfold before her."

"I trust we won't have to have this talk again? The outcome may not be so pleasant next time."

"My term would be extended by how long?"

The judge shrugs his shoulders. "You died before your time doing something foolish. Honestly Sam, black diamond runs are well marked for a reason. It's that same impetuous nature that is getting you in trouble again."

"I do feel like I've learned a lot since being here," Sam interjects.

God smiles down at him. "Sam, I feel the work of angels is not only a privilege, but a form of heroism. You are here to serve humans and keep them from making similar mistakes. When you have learned all of your lessons -- restraint, judgement, and unselfishness -- then you will be returned to live out the rest of your days. I'm afraid you'll have to remain in this body though. You did make a mess of the last one."

"Sorry," he says sheepishly. "But this one's fine with me." He careens his neck to see past God and gaze in a mirror in order to place a wayward strand of hair back into place. Satisfied with what he sees -- a strong jawline, prominent cheekbones and a cleft in his chin that deepens when his smile flashes -- the golden haired angel awaits God's orders.

"Oh my, look at the time! I have a board meeting to get to. There are so many problems in the middle east that need to be addressed. Good talk, Sam. Go back to Earth and back to work. We'll reconvene soon."

"Uh yeah, you too, God." Sam ran a hand through his hair. He dodged a bullet so to speak, and exhaled audibly with relief. The landscape shifted and blurred. A bright light flashed and Sam found himself in modern attire -- beach board shorts of a bright red, flip flops, no shirt. His tanned skin accentuated his chiseled chest and tight abs, and more than a couple of girls admired his physique as he made his way down the wooden staircase from the parking lot on Pacific Coast Highway to the soft, white sand of El Matador Beach in Malibu just a few hours after sunrise.

Sam placed his hands on the deck of a blue structure rising majestically from the sand and easily pressed himself upward. Taking a moment to survey his domain, he inhaled the refreshing salt air and cleared his mind, preparing for work. Unlocking the cabinet, he located his buoy, prominently emblazoned with the word, "GUARD," and stood at the ready, prepared to watch over the beach-goers.

# # #

Chapter Two

"What do you think?" Angeline did an elaborate twirl letting the sheer fabric of her beach cover-up flair out before coming to a stop and striking a pose. With a hand on her hip, she jutted out a curvy haunch, threw back her shoulders and sucked in her cheeks, mimicking an overly confident runway model.

"So cute! Is that one of your new ones?" Her friend, Taylor, beamed her approval. "I didn't know you were doing cover-ups."

"Still mainly bikinis, but I thought it couldn't hurt to add a few new things. Want to see the new line?" Angeline tossed the cover-up aside revealing her bathing suit beneath. "So give me your honest opinion. Every bathing suit is supposed to be sexy, but I'm trying to reach out to the female surfer crowd so I'm going for athletic also. Does this say functionality as well?" she asked, giving her body a wave of her hands.

She was wearing light blue boy shorts that ended just below the curve of her butt and sat below her bellybutton. A sleeveless, crop top featuring a high neckline offered a hipper alternative to the traditional bikini top. Both were made out of thin spandex that hugged the curves, but kept the water and sun at bay. A prominent sunflower design was strategically placed on her behind while another sat front and center on her top, the perfect embodiment of Angeline's exuberance and sunny disposition

"You've got mad design skills plus the perfect beach body to show them off. But, have you got a business plan?"

Angeline fluttered her hand back and forth in the universal motion that basically translated to sorta, maybe, not really. "I've got a plan," she hedged. "But whether hanging out at the beach in my suit can be considered a business plan remains to be seen."

"At least it's a start. Shall we go?" Taylor grabbed her beach bag containing a towel, suncream, and a romance novel.

"Is that all you're taking? No boogie board, skimboard, nothing for the water?"

Taylor patted her paperback and then planted a kiss on the cover, which depicted a muscled, shirtless man. "I've got a book. What else do I need?"

Angeline shot her friend a fake pout. "It's just that my plan sort of involves us learning to surf. I can't exactly launch a surfer line without being able to walk the walk."

"Or drown in the water?"

Angeline fluttered her hand again as if swatting a fly. "Of course I'm not going to drown. I'm going to get lessons."

"Wait a minute, Angel. I don't think that's such a good idea. You and water...not a good combination. Remember what happened at summer camp?"

Angeline rolled her eyes. "We were twelve! Besides, I think I've learned not to eat a double cheeseburger before going swimming."

"And what about last summer?" Taylor prompted.

Angeline begrudgingly shrugged her shoulders. "So, I might have become a little concerned when the water got rough. That can happen to anyone."

Raising her eyebrows, Taylor shot her friend a most decidedly 'I'm not buying it' look.

"Okay, in all fairness to me, you have to admit that those waves were intense."

"Angel, we were in a community pool with a splashing nine-year-old."

Angeline grabbed her bag, opened the door and headed out in a show of defiance. "I'm not buying it. He had to have been the devil and that water was coming at me with the force of a fire hydrant."

Taylor smiled with amusement at her friend. When Angeline put her mind to something there was no stopping her.

Embodying this thought she called out, "So, you comin' or what?"

"Yeah, let's hit the beach."

Taylor closed the door and followed her friend to the cream and white convertible Mini Cooper that stood in the driveway, its back seat already loaded up with Angeline's new surf board along with bathing suit samples and mock-up catalogs with even more designs.

# # #

Chapter Three

The air was warming up as the sun rose higher in the sky. The first of the day's beach-goers arrived, trudging over sand dunes to get closer to the ocean. El Matador's caves offered a shady respite for parents who struggled to carry blankets, umbrellas, lunch coolers and children's sand toys. One mother waited patiently for her son to catch up, but his trek was slowed by the increasing amount of sand that filled his little shoes.

"Take them off," his mother called out.

"The sand is too hot," her little boy retorted.

With nobody in the water yet, Sam offered his help. "Want a lift?"

"Sure!" the boy beamed.

Sam bent down and the little boy scrambled up his back. Sam heaved him upwards onto his shoulders, then proceeded to walk him to where his mother had set up camp for the day's outing.

As he turned to return to his lifeguard tower, Sam noticed his co-worker had arrived for the day. He gave an easy wave and then jogged back.

"Hey, you must be Sam; I'm Evan." Also dressed in the lifeguard's uniform of red shorts and nothing else except his buoy, Evan extended a tanned arm and the two men shook hands.

"Nice to meet you. Seems like it's going to be a pretty quiet day," Sam said looking out to the ocean.

A smile crept over Evan's face. "Oh, I wouldn't count my chickens just yet."

He jerked his thumb over his shoulder and motioned to the staircase that led down to the beach from the parking lot. There on the top, two young women were making their way down, one was dropping her belongings every other step of the journey.

"So she's clumsy, but certainly not trouble," Sam commented.

"You don't recognize her?"

Sam squinted his eyes, but her floppy hat blocked her face. "Should I? She doesn't seem to have the...walking skills of an actress or model."

Evan put his arm around Sam's shoulder. "Take a closer look."

Sam squinted his eyes, trying to figure out what Evan was implying.

"She's not trouble in the usual sense as in causing a ruckus. Just trouble for you, my friend."

Sam's baffled look quickly turned to adoration and then astonishment as he spied Angeline's smiling face as she made her way past his lifeguard tower.

"You know her? You know about me? How is that possible?" Sam's mind was a whir of questions as he searched Evan's face for answers all the while keeping an eye on Angeline, needing to know where she was parking her blanket for the day.

Evan gave him an amused look. "Wait a minute? You think you're the only guardian angel?"

"Well...no. I assumed there were others, but what are the chances of actually meeting one?"

Evan pointed a bit farther up the beach. "You see those lifeguards?" he motioned to where the next lifeguard tower stood. "Tower #24?"

"Yeah?"

"And that way..." Evan nodded in the other direction, "...is tower #26."

"Your point?"

"We're all lifeguards. That's what the humans call us, anyway."

A look that combined shock, surprise and sudden recognition lit up Sam's face. "You mean *all* lifeguards are guardian angels?"

"Bingo."

"That makes so much sense now," Sam admitted. "Not to be weird, but those two guys at tower #24 have bodies that look air-brushed and I don't remember having abs like this before...," Sam paused, not really wanting to relive the moment that sent him to the great beyond and then back again. "I guess that's why it's so easy to run in dry sand. We sort of...float."

"I wouldn't go that far. Glide, maybe."

Sam nodded as if digesting the thought. "Anyway, it hasn't been easy for me. Lots of rules go with these wings."

Evan took a moment to grab ahold of the top of the tower, letting his body hang so he could engage in a few impromptu pull-ups, as if his body weight was featherlight. "I'll let you in on a secret...one that isn't meant to get around. Lifeguards...guardian angels...whatever you want to call us, it's not easy. Sure, it's an honor to be chosen, but it comes with a lot of temptation, maybe more than you imagine."

At that moment, two beautiful girls walked by the tower and gazed longingly at Evan and Sam. "You see?"

As if magnifying his point, another two girls in barely there bikinis sauntered past and then one, as if compelled, turned and stopped, smiling up at Evan and Sam. "Hi," she said seductively.

In his professional voice, friendly, but removed, Evan answered. "Hello. You remember to be careful out there today."

"What if I were to stay up there with you?"

"Sorry. That's against regulations."

The girl pouted slightly before turning away and walking off with her friend.

Sam turned to Evan. "So I take it you've never been involved with a human during your time here?"

Evan shook his head. "It's easier for me to give advice than take it."

"Really?"

Evan nodded his head with a bit of shame.

"Do you regret it?" Sam asked, his eyes scanning the beach in search of Angeline.

Evan lowered his voice to just a whisper. "Absolutely not."

Sam studied his expression and took in a look that seemed to convey a bit of emptiness as if there was a gap in his heart that someone once filled. "You want to talk about it?"

Evan shook his head. "It's a long story and one that I need some time to get over. I'm getting better. I try to throw myself into my work."

"Is it working?" Sam asked, not relishing the idea that his fate may be the same as Evan's.

"It's definitely harder when you notice the couples holding hands, the girls who offer an admiring glance. But, then I remember that mistakes don't go unpunished. I ended up having an entire year added to my time."

Sam seemed to take it all in, weighing his own feelings toward Angeline. It was futile to pursue her and make his life more difficult. As long as she didn't notice him, he would be safe. "But what if your girl were here...right now. What would you do?" Sam asked.

"I'd have no choice. I'd love her all over again. In a heartbeat."

"Did anyone ever tell you that you're shit at giving advice?" Sam nodded dreamily, his thoughts once again on Angeline. "I was told not to meddle."

"How's that working out for you?"

"I got called in for a talk with the boss just yesterday. I promised it wouldn't happen again."

"Maybe she'll just be here for the day and then tomorrow you can put your mind to other things," Evan offered.

"Somehow, I think not. I get the feeling that this is one of the afterlife's little tests."

Evan scanned the beach with his binoculars while still talking with Sam. "Just remember, you can't change your human's destiny, but don't confuse our bylaws with your oath to protect. You can't always hide your head in the sand, no pun intended. Especially when something like this is happening."

"Like what?" The moment he uttered the words, Sam instinctively turned to find Angeline engaged in a conversation with one of the local surfers. His light brown hair hung to his shoulders and was pulled back in a ponytail. He had a slighter build than Sam, but despite his body's trim appearance, he was muscular. No doubt it was from his time in the water. Sam reached for the binoculars to get a closer look at him and spied a tattoo of a curling wave emblazoned on his upper arm. He also noticed how the guy was leaning in closely to Angeline and even though Sam was an angel, it made his blood boil.

Evan glanced at Sam. "I've got one week left on my term; word on the clouds is that you're supposed to be out of here in one month. We gonna get busy or what?"

Sam nodded and then extended his fist, which Evan promptly bumped and the two headed out for their first patrol of the morning.

# # #

Chapter Four

Sam and Evan were jogging about a half mile from their tower close to the water's edge when Evan pointed to the sand just in time for Sam to sidestep the jellyfish that had washed ashore.

"It's dead, but the venom can still be active," Evan reminded.

As if magnifying his point, a woman flagged them down, her little boy was sitting by her side crying loudly. Sam recognized him as the boy he had carried across the sand.

"I wish you had carried me longer," the boy wept.

"Me too, buddy," Sam said bending his head lower to examine the boy's foot. "Can I take a closer look?"

The boy nodded and extended his leg. Sam turned to his mother. "Vinegar is a known treatment. It will stop the stinging. We can carry him back to the tower if you want to follow."

"Yes, please," she answered.

Evan turned to Sam. "You take care of the boy and I'll come back and post some warning signs." Then addressing the boy, he added, "You're going to be fine. My friend here is going to make it stop hurting."

"What about the needles?" the boy asked.

"I know it feels like needles, but jellyfish have tentacles and they don't leave them on you. We're going to get you all fixed up," Sam reassured.

"No, real needles. See?"

The boy pointed to a nearby pile of seaweed where two hypodermic needles were buried among the kelp. Sam reached into his first aid bag to retrieve a pair of gloves along with a plastic sampling bag. After putting on the gloves, he carefully retrieved the needles and placed them into the bags.

"Have you seen more like this?" he asked the boy. The little boy earnestly shook his head.

"What do you make of this?" Sam asked Evan.

"First the jellyfish, now this. We definitely need to clean up this beach."

# # #

Chapter Five

Angeline looked up at the young surfer and couldn't help but be taken in by his carefree attitude. What was it about guys who acted like they couldn't give a damn that made a woman want them all the more? Charmed by his bohemian mannerisms as well as his bad boy good looks -- hair that was a little too long and fell into his eyes, the tattoo on his arm and toned legs from the hours he spent in the water.

She never expected to find a teacher so quickly, nor had she considered taking those lessons from someone who wasn't actually affiliated with a school, but then she rationalized why not really experience the surf culture from an actual local? The more Angeline considered it, the more she found herself thinking that surf lessons sounded like a mighty fine idea right now. The water was warm at this time of year, making wetsuits unnecessary. She smiled to herself and sent a little thank you to the man upstairs as she took in the surfer's broad chest.

"I cross my heart. I won't let anything happen to you." He reached out and brushed a lock of hair from her eyes and held her stare a bit longer than someone who had just a passing interest.

"You swear it?" Angeline replied, the reality of what she was about to do settling in. "I tend to be a little accident prone."

"Trust me. The waves are mellow and the water's warm. What have you got to lose?"

He came across a bit strong, but then again, confidence could be a turn-on. Angeline weighed the pros and cons, and unable to come up with a good reason to say no to this heartbreaker who was giving her so much attention, and finally replied, "Give me a sec to tell my friend."

#

"You're a natural," the surfer told Angeline as he balanced her on the board, his hand on her lower back.

She laughed. "I don't think lying on my stomach qualifies me for all that praise."

He nuzzled her ear, taking her lobe between his teeth. The feeling sent chills of surprise up Angeline's core. He was sexy and dangerous. "You are so hot."

Angeline shook her head.

"What? It's true. What I want to do to you and that tight ass of yours."

Angeline wasn't used to a guy being so bold, but then again, she wasn't used to being in such a precarious state and still feeling so safe. The waves were picking up, but the surfer ensured that she stayed on top of her board. He guided her board onto shore and then helped her back out again. It was exhilarating, intoxicating, and even when his hands ran down the back of her thighs, she found herself falling under his spell.

"So, about my designs," she hedged, trying to steer the conversation away from such intimate musings.

"Babe, if your other stuff is anything like this suit you're wearing..." he said, daring to slide his finger under the material that gathered at her upper thigh and just below her bottom, "then, you will be selling these like hotcakes."

"Can you introduce me to your surfing rep?"

"I think that can be arranged. But, they're more likely to take you seriously if you can surf. I mean, you are trying to push a surf line, after all. You're not opposed to spending more time with me, are you?" he asked and then ran his hand down her back and over her rear.

Angeline felt a chill run down her spine, both from his advances as well as the implication. She felt nervous and excited all at once and confusion was settling into her brain. She had thought learning to surf would help her get in with that crowd, but now that she was actually doing it, fear was forming in her gut as well. But no sooner did one side of her brain warn her away when the other told her to stop being so cautious and go for her dreams.

The surfer had told her that he was sponsored by one of the major surf wear companies and given the skill in which he rode the waves, she had no reason not to believe him. The only question in Angeline's mind was what she would have to do to keep him interested in her without sacrificing her morals. He had made it clear that a professional relationship was not what he was after.

When his mouth found hers, she relented and kissed him back. He no sooner tied his board's leash to hers and then jumped on the back of hers, straddling the board directly behind Angeline. "The water's calm. This is the time that I like to sit back and admire the beauty around me." He ran his hand over Angeline's back. "Isn't this nice?"

"Uh huh," she said, albeit a bit uneasily.

"We've got probably a good fifteen minutes before the swells change again. How should we pass the time?" he asked rhetorically.

"Are you sure we're not too far out?" Angeline looked around and noticed that the other surfers seemed to have given up for the day.

"Nah, it's just quiet because we've got baby waves right now. Come here." With Angeline still on her stomach, he pressed his arms on either side of her and hoisted himself between her legs, moving her thighs open with his knees. Normally, Angeline would never allow herself to be in such a position, but there wasn't really any place for him to be, aside from his own board. And, truth be told, Angeline did feel safer with him closer to guide her. Plus, she reasoned that nothing too inappropriate could happen with them out in the open.

But when he leaned forward, she felt his hardness between her legs. Her body and mind were in direct opposition with each other. She immediately tensed with the knowledge that he and his moves were too fast for her liking. But it had been ages since she was with anyone and she couldn't help starting to feel aroused in spite of her misgivings.

As if the gods above could sense her confusion, a huge wave started to build behind them. "Looks like our play time is coming to a close. Hang on," he said and to her relief, he got out of the sexually charged position and managed to expertly guide them to shore.

# # #

Chapter Six

"I can't believe that guy!" Sam fumed. "He had his hands all over her."

"It's a little tough to keep someone balanced on a surfboard if you don't have your hands on them," Evan hedged.

"Well, she's different...she's off-limits."

Evan shot him a look. "What do you mean? I said to keep an eye on her. I meant in case she's not a strong swimmer, not for any other reason. You're not meddling, are you?"

Sam ran a hand through his hair and then shook his head, removing some of the salt water while showing his displeasure. "Of course not."

"Then, why don't I believe you? Did you not learn anything from my sob story? Tell me, just how well do you know that girl?"

"She's working to be a clothing designer, specializing in beach wear. She lives in the Valley. Her name is Angeline...Angel. And, I might be in love with her."

"Sounds like you know a lot about her." Evan nodded to himself, trying to find the right way to say what was on his mind. Finally, he just went for it. "Dude, you are treading in very deep water...sorry, another lifeguard pun. If you pursue her, not only will your time be extended, but your heart will end up broken."

"Not with this one. She has a heart of gold."

# # #

As the week progressed, Sam discovered the mixed blessing that keeping tabs on Angeline was getting easier. He no longer had to follow her to coffee houses or cafes as she was spending regular time on the beach.

That was the good news. The bad was that now there was no getting her off of his mind. Worse yet, she was spending her time with some other guy...a guy whom Sam didn't trust and certainly didn't deem worthy enough to carry Angeline's beach towel, let alone become her boyfriend.

As evidence of his gnawing concern about the guy, Sam spotted him chatting up another pretty girl in the parking lot as he headed into work for the day. Sam could tell from their body language -- surfer dude leaning in close and casually placing a lock of beach babe's hair behind her ear -- that some serious flirting was taking place. Sam looked over at him and scowled, but the guy didn't notice as he was too absorbed in his conversation with the babe in the bikini.

Sam didn't want to seem like a pervert, but there was something odd about his interaction with the girl. Initially, he seemed to be seriously checking her out, but his body language changed when the girl seemed to be asking for something. She kept making the cross-my-heart sign and then held her hands up in prayer as if pleading with the surfer for something. Deciding that his duty as a lifeguard applied to everyone, not just as guardian angel to Angeline, Sam grabbed his binoculars to catch a better look at what was going down between the two of them.

Training his binoculars on the girl he watched as she took the surfer's hand and then immediately placed her hand within it and retrieved what looked like a folded piece of tinfoil. She pocketed the small package and then gave him a kiss on the cheek. She ducked into her car for a minute, before coming out and rejoining the surfer. The two then headed down to the beach hand in hand. The whole scene unfolded in mere seconds, but it was enough to deepen Sam's distrust of the guy.

Sam stomped over to the lifeguard tower and heaved himself up and onto the platform where Evan was already getting out their gear. He handed Sam a pair of binoculars and a life preserver before he noticed the tension seeping from his colleague.

"You okay?"

"Yep," Sam said curtly, emphasizing the "P".

Evan narrowed his eyes and took a quick look around to try and figure out what had Sam in a tizzy. A lyrical laugh drew his attention to the girl who was now rubbing oil over the surfer's shoulders and instinctively Evan knew he had spotted the source of Sam's torment.

"What? I'd think you'd be glad that he found a distraction from Angeline."

Sam shook his head. "He didn't. He's just playing the field and she doesn't know it. Take a look." He handed Evan the binoculars, indicating he should scan the beach. One look and a frown crossed Evan's tanned features. "That girl who's with him..."

"Yeah, what about her?"

"I recognize her. A couple of months back, she nearly drowned after deciding that it was a good idea to do a few rounds of cocaine before surfing. I thought she cleaned up her act, but now I'm thinking she just didn't have a supplier...until now."

"Him?"

Evan's expression was grim. "Could be."

"So why can't we detain him and call the authorities? Jeez, I don't want Angeline caught up with this guy. She has no idea what he is," Sam exclaimed, stress seeping from his voice.

"And neither do we, truthfully. He's smart. He lies low and then after the heat is off him, he comes back into action. The authorities haven't been able to pin anything on him. I just suggest you do what we do best."

Sam shook his head, knowing where the conversation was going. "I'm supposed to just watch. Be there just in case. And take care of her when she falls."

Evan nodded solemnly. "It's a tougher job than it appears."

"You're telling me."

# # #

Chapter Seven

Angeline was waxing up her surfboard, trying to look busy, but it was obvious that she was waiting for someone...for him. She kept turning in the direction of the lifeguard station, which stood at the pedestrian entrance to the beach. Every time her beautiful face turned toward Sam he would smile to himself, just because seeing her did that to him.

"I swear, if he hurts her...if she falls for him...Over my dead body will I let that happen," Sam proclaimed to Evan.

"Uh...Sam?" Evan winced, not wanting to state the obvious.

Sam gave a wave of his hand. "You know what I mean. She deserves better."

"Just checking, buddy. So long as you remember the rules."

"Rules..." Sam muttered, the word itself leaving a bad taste in his mouth.

"Hey, maybe things are looking up for you. Check it out."

Angeline was making her way up from the shoreline having stood her surfboard in the sand just before the rock point. A few scattered houses stood proud above her and to her left was Sam's lifeguard tower, where she seemed to be headed.

Sam immediately jumped down from the tower. "I'll handle this," he called up.

"Will you now? I would've never guessed it," Evan said breezily, a smile plastered to his knowing face.

In spite of the soft sand, Angeline's strong, lean legs carried her across it quickly. To Sam, her graceful movements were like those of an angel -- his very own angel -- until she stumbled and landed on her butt. He jumped from the tower and ran to her immediately. "Can I help you?" he asked politely, extending a hand to her.

She accepted his hand and stared up at him, squinting from the sunlight.

"Here, let me help you up." In one easy motion, Sam had her on her feet and she fell into his arms. He could have easily released her. There was no sign of any injury to her ankle or leg, but he didn't want to let her go just yet. He didn't know if he would ever have the chance to hold her in his arms again. When she gave him a smile, slightly shy and tinged with a bit of awkwardness, he knew he had to let her go. "Did you need any help?" he asked her again.

"Yeah, I was hoping..."

Sam's mind imagined a million wonderful scenarios she could say. Things like: "Could you help me count every grain of sand on the beach? Could you stay past your work hours and watch the sunset with me?"

Instead, she said, "My surfing instructor hasn't shown up yet and I was just wondering..." her gaze now going to the ocean, "do you know if the swells are supposed to stay around this size for awhile?"

Sam looked out to the right of where she had planted her surfboard, an area known as Surfer's Point, where the waves were slightly bigger and the beach slightly more narrow with rocky bits that scattered the shoreline.

"You're safer trying down there," he pointed to the opposite side of the beach, where a few young kids were boogie boarding. "Just until you get your bearings."

Angeline gave a noticeable pout. "I've been riding the kiddie waves all week. I was really hoping to test out what I've learned...but as I said, my instructor seems to be AWOL. Hey, do you think you could take me?"

Sam looked up to the tower at Evan, unsure how to proceed. He would have done anything to say yes right on the spot, but that would certainly get him into trouble. Then again, to send her out alone was irresponsible and could endanger her safety. Knowing exactly how Sam's mind was playing a game of angel versus devil, Evan shook his head slightly to which Sam rolled his eyes at his new friend, but nodded recognition nonetheless.

"I'd love to, really I would. But, I'm on duty."

"Oh, of course. That was silly of me. Hey, I'm sorry I bothered you," Angeline said as she started to turn away from the tower.

"You're not a bother. Come by anytime. I've got sandwiches!" he called out as she headed back down the beach.

Evan smirked at him. "I've got sandwiches? Now that's an original pick-up line."

Sam ran a hand through his golden hair. "Tell me I didn't really say that."

"Just wondering...did that kind of line work when you were alive?"

Sam smiled in spite of his embarrassment. "Actually, girls found me to be quite cute and charming."

As if validating his point, Angeline looked over her shoulder at Sam, but seeing him still watching her, she immediately turned back and continued walking to her spot on the beach.

Evan raised his eyes skyward. "Trouble. That's all I'm gonna say."

Placing his arms behind his head and leaning back against the lifeguard tower, Sam surveyed his domain over the pristine Malibu beach, taking in the sun, surf, and the beautiful swaying of Angeline's hips. "That's the type of trouble that makes life...and the afterlife...worth living."

Chapter Eight

Ever since becoming an angel, Sam never experienced discomfort. No headaches, no back aches, in fact no aches or pains of any sort. Except where his heart was concerned. Heartache had become a constant in his life and as he approached Angeline, wondering if the powers that be were looking down at him with disapproval, he decided at that moment it was worth remaining an angel for all of eternity if it meant spending even one afternoon with his own angel.

The sight of Angeline lying on a blanket in the sand and wearing a white bikini took his breath away. She indeed looked the part of an angel as she lay with her blonde curls fanned out, her eyes closed, and seemingly at total peace. He didn't dare speak. He couldn't bring himself to disturb her.

But sensing a presence, she looked up at him. "You're here!" Angeline placed a hand over her eyes to shield them from the sunlight that always seemed to shine a little brighter in Sam's presence, and sent him a look of true gratitude simply because he was near. She bounded upwards and did a little jump for joy. It was endearing and made Sam fall even harder for her.

"So, you changed your mind about taking me out?"

As Sam took in her perfect figure and admired her personality that exuded nothing but positive energy, he thought about how much he would like to take her out to dinner, spend an evening talking with her, and maybe even kiss those perfect lips that he found himself staring at. When her demeanor seemed to change, he suddenly realized that he had been lost in his own thoughts and hadn't answered her.

"Or not," she noted sadly. "I'm sorry. I didn't mean to put you on the spot."

"No! You didn't. It's just that I'm actually on my patrol of the beach."

She nodded sadly. "I feel like an idiot."

"You shouldn't because I'd love to go surfing with you once my shift is over."

Suddenly a strong hand clapped Sam on the shoulder. "That's mighty friendly of you, but I've got her."

Sam looked up to see the surfer taking a dominating stance with his legs spread, attempting to take up space the way men do when they want to show who has the biggest balls. The surfer moved closer to Angeline and brushed a finger under her chin. It was a move akin to something one would do to a pet and it majorly pissed off Sam. He hated the idea of this guy touching Angeline even with that one finger let alone going surfing with her and having his hands all over her body.

Angeline looked up equally surprised. "You had me thinking that you weren't going to show up today."

"I just got a little delayed with a potential client. You know I wouldn't miss our date, Honey," the surfer drawled. It made Sam sick and he narrowed his eyes at the surfer as if to tell him that he wasn't fooling him with that line. But Angeline seemed to eat it up. Still, she had the good manners to look to Sam before accepting her pre-arranged date.

"Can we take a rain check?" Her expression revealed that at least a part of her was disappointed that her original plans were still intact.

"Of course. You be careful," Sam said, as much to the surfer who was entrusted with Angeline's safety.

Remembering his orders from none other than God himself, Sam knew that he was obligated to let this play out. God had spent many hours lecturing him about the need for humans to date and experience the good as well as the bad. *You must let the process as well as her life unfold.* Sam crossed his arms in front of his chest, feeling both angry and defeated as he recalled God's words to him.

The surfer picked up Angeline's board and easily balanced it over his head while placing a hand on her waist and leading her to the water. "See ya, lifeguard," he called over his shoulder before turning to give Sam a knowing wink.

They had each other's numbers -- both knowing that Angeline was a girl worth fighting for -- but Sam was helpless to step into the ring. He had to just hope that this guy would do right by her.

# # #

Angeline had finished her surf lesson, but to Sam's chagrin, she had followed the surfer into the parking lot. It was time for Sam to go home, but he couldn't. He just couldn't leave, not with Angeline sitting in that guy's dilapidated van. Thus far, they had just been talking in the front seat, but he wasn't comfortable leaving her here alone...or at least alone with him.

"You headed out?" Evan asked as he put the last of their rescue equipment inside the tower.

"Soon," Sam replied, trying to sound casual.

"Listen, if you help me haul our boards to the shed you can steal a closer look at your girl. I know you want to go up those stairs again to sneak a peak. Come on," Evan referred to the city lifeguard's storage unit, conveniently located just a few spots away from where the surfer had parked.

"I'm on it." Sam jumped off the tower into the sand easily, grabbed the first board and headed up the wooden stairs to the parking lot, but he stopped dead in his tracks the moment he got to the last step. "Great," he muttered to Evan, who was just a step behind him.

Angeline was engaged in a lip lock with the surfer, his hands were on her back, pulling her in closer to him.

"You could pound on the window and tell 'em about the city indecency laws or parking after 6 p.m. being prohibited." Evan shrugged, knowing the sight of the couple was killing Sam.

Sam just shook his head. "Unless she's in danger, my hands are tied."

Evan patted him on the back before heading in the direction of his own car. "Good man...er, I mean, good guardian. You're doing the right thing. Hey, you wanna grab a beer? There's no guardian angel rule against that."

"I'm just gonna hang here. Until she leaves, I'm here."

Evan headed out and Sam busied himself with mundane clean-up tasks in an attempt to not look like he was spying on Angeline. Watching her with him was the last thing he wanted, especially when it appeared as if their kissing was intensifying. And then suddenly a cold wind blew in, capturing Sam's attention.

He stopped what he was doing and didn't shy away from turning to look directly at the van. It was then that he saw the surfer untie Angeline's bathing suit top and run his hands over her back, but she immediately batted them away and grabbed frantically for the ties.

Her expression was angry as she sat with decidedly more distance between them. Sam could see them talking, or actually what appeared more like arguing.

"Well, I'm sorry you feel that way," she said and jumped out of the van.

He rolled down the window and shouted out to her. "You want me to get your designs seen? Then I suggest you stop being such a tease."

Angeline just shook her head, unable to find the words for a comeback. The passenger door had barely shut when he turned on the engine and peeled away. She looked after the van with an expression that revealed her disappointment, and when she turned to see Sam watching her, it changed again to embarrassment.

"You okay?" he asked, moving toward her. His heart ached just taking in her expression and he wanted to hold her, to tell her that she deserved so much better.

"Yeah. I'm fine. We just seem to have a difference of opinion about our relationship."

Sam nodded and noticed that she was shivering. "Here," he said wrapping a towel around her shoulders.

"Thank you."

They stood in silence for a moment, the sun slowly making its descent and turning the sky a bright shade of pink.

"You get beautiful sunsets in Malibu," she commented.

"The view is even better from atop the tower. Do you have a minute?"

When she nodded happily, Sam offered his hand, which she accepted. They reached the tower and Sam cupped his hands together for Angeline to step up. "Just place your foot on my hands. I'll lift you."

She did as he said and with ease he elevated her until she was level with the tower's platform. Her attention was brought to his strong shoulders and chest, which allowed him to pull himself up as if it were nothing. "You cold?"

"A little," she admitted.

He immediately went to take off his lifeguard's jacket to which she protested his gallantry. "I couldn't. You're gonna get cold."

"I'm used to the beach air. I usually stay until after sunset. It's my favorite time here. It's just so peaceful."

Angeline bit her lower lip. "Maybe I should go. I've caused enough disturbance for one day," she said and moved to jump down.

Without thinking, Sam quickly grabbed her hand. "Please stay. It's nice having the company."

At that moment, two dolphins jumped above the waves and then disappeared again. "Did you see that?" Angeline exclaimed.

She settled herself back down next to Sam and he shivered involuntarily with the proximity to her body.

"Here, you have to take this back," she indicated the jacket.

"Don't be silly. I've got an idea for a compromise..." he reached for an oversized beach towel. "We can share. Put your legs over mine," he instructed to which she obliged. He wrapped the towel around the both of them, enclosing them into a warm cocoon. His arms found their way around her waist and he held her close. She leaned into him and felt the warmth that he radiated.

Her cheek rested on his shoulder, bringing her mouth so dangerously close to his own. If he just bent his head, even in the slightest, he could kiss her. How he desperately wanted to.

"Maybe you shouldn't see him again." A sudden cold breeze blew its warning at Sam's comment. He glanced toward the heavens and scowled, but hearing her sigh, he immediately turned and touched his forehead to hers. They sat like that, not moving, not speaking, until she whispered back.

"Maybe I shouldn't."

# # #

Chapter Nine

Angeline returned to her apartment later than she expected to find Taylor making her signature dinner of grilled mahi mahi with pineapple salsa.

"Oh my god, that smells amazing. Is there enough for me to sneak a little piece?"

Taylor handed her a plate and placed a healthy portion onto it. "You don't have to sneak it. You know I always make enough for you. But, I would have thought you'd have eaten already. Where have you been?" she said with a critical glance in Angeline's direction.

"Nowhere...just hanging at the beach, well actually in Kai's van."

"Kai?"

"The guy giving me surf lessons."

Taylor wrinkled her nose and turned her mouth downward. "His van. Really Angeline."

"No! It's not like that. Well, he probably would have liked it to be like that, but it wasn't. We just talked."

Taylor was studying psychology and had learned in a recent class that most people have the uncontrollable habit of glancing upwards just before telling a lie. She wasn't buying Angeline's story...not one bit of it. "Just talked?"

"Okay, maybe we kissed a little. But I swear, that's it. Especially since...well, nothing."

"No way. You're not going to leave that sentence floating in the air. Angeline, if you want seconds," she pointed to the frying pan, "than you better dish."

"He's cute and everything, but he's totally on the make. One minute he was leaning in to kiss me and I kissed him back and then it was like dealing with an octopus. I swear he was everywhere all at once. So I pulled back and suggested we grab some dinner and his response was that he wasn't hungry and he'd see me tomorrow."

"He wasn't hungry." Taylor scoffed and rolled her eyes. "What guy says that? Come on, Angeline."

Angeline took a bite of her food and washed it down with a sip of white wine. "Maybe he was just tired. We had been surfing all day."

"You're not going out with him again, are you?" Taylor's voice had an edge to it.

"It's not like we're going out."

"My point exactly. If you were really going out I wouldn't be acting like your mother."

"Taylor, you sound just like that cute lifeguard."

"What? And when were you going to tell me about him?" Taylor wiggled her eyebrows at Angeline.

"I don't know why, but I felt like I was caught with my hand in the cookie jar. He saw us at the worst moment. Kai was getting a bit too frisky, my top had come untied..."

"What?!" Taylor said a bit more loudly this time.

Angeline nodded and closed her eyes as if to ward off another look of disappointment being cast her way. "Yeah, he's sweet, but I don't think he's interested. I mean, maybe he is, but I get the idea that he's not allowed to date people at work."

"People at work?! He works at the beach. That puts a lot of people off limits," Taylor added.

Angeline shrugged her shoulders. "He's just...different. A little standoffish, but then caring as well. I don't know. Anyway, I still need these surfing lessons," Angeline added carefully.

"Oh Angeline!"

"Listen, I know he's not boyfriend material. Unless I'm into a no strings attached sort of thing. But he's got that hot bad boy vibe and besides, nobody else is asking me out."

"Nobody as in...the cute lifeguard?"

Angeline released a small, but forced laugh, a sound that masked her own disappointment. "Why is it so hard to find a guy who wants to be there for the long haul?"

Taylor tipped her own glass to Angeline's. "Well, let's toast to finding him."

# # #

The next day, Sam arrived at the beach far earlier than his shift demanded. He took off toward the shoreline at a jog, wanting to clear his head before work began. He couldn't get his mind off Angeline and had spent most of the night worrying about what may or may not have happened between her and the surfer had he not turned up.

As he headed toward the point, he sidestepped rocks and still more jellyfish that had washed ashore, avoiding stepping on them and the sting that would surely occur as a result. It was then that he made the conscious choice to devote himself to his job. Not only because God demanded it, but it was just easier.

Like the venom of a jellyfish, Angeline had gotten under his skin and he needed to save his heart from being burned. He might not be able to be *with* her, but he could certainly be there *for* her. His strides were long and fast, his movements quickly changing from jogging to running.

And then, it was as if his own thoughts made her materialize. About a quarter mile up the beach he saw her. The normal beach-goers had yet to arrive. With the exception of the die-hard surfers who showed up at the crack of dawn, the beach was empty. She stood in a yoga pose, one hand holding her leg behind her, the other proudly pointed forward. Her white cover-up floated behind her in the early breeze. She looked positively ethereal and without any trace of the clumsiness he had come to love.

As his footsteps approached, she stumbled out of the pose and looked over at him. Upon seeing it was Sam, a blush crossed her features. "I was just stretching," she said sounding somewhat embarrassed at being caught. "This can be hard work," she motioned to her board, which had a circle of polish on it, and immediately bent down to continue buffing it up.

"That's a very nice board," he said breezily, trying to sound casual in spite of feeling a bevy of nerves. "How did it treat you yesterday?"

"Well, I just bought it so we're still getting to know each other," Angeline replied, obviously proud of her new purchase. "Never expected to love surfing as much as I do."

"What made you get into it?"

"It's kind of silly," Angeline said shyly. "I'm sure I look like a total goofball out there. My surfing skills aren't exactly refined." She paused and licked her lower lip. Sam noticed the sudden change in her mood from sunny to downcast. He lowered himself down on one knee to be closer to her.

"Is everything alright?"

She gave a little shrug to her shoulders before hesitantly replying. "After yesterday, I kind of feel like a dork both in the water...and out. I hope you don't...think poorly of me. You know, after what you saw."

Sam noticed that she was twirling a curl of her blonde hair around one of her fingers and fidgeting by making designs in the sand with one foot. Even without makeup, she was beautiful yet totally unaware of her natural appeal.

"Trust me, that would be impossible."

She beamed at him, taking in his handsome features and being thankful for the kind attention he lauded on her. If only he were bolder and asked her out. Or maybe, he was taken. Perhaps the city had a strict rule about lifeguards not fraternizing with the people on their beach. The thoughts ran through her mind and each time, she wished that the rules were different.

Bringing the attention back to her once more, Sam asked, "Have you always wanted to be a surfer?"

"Well actually, I'm trying to be a bathing suit designer, hopefully for the surfing crowd. I just figured learning to actually surf went with the territory."

"Is that one of your designs? It's very...becoming." He indicating the bathing suit that she wore as his eyes scanned her perfect figure. This suit was of a mint green color that brought out her incredible eyes, which were of a slightly darker green. A light fern leaf imprint graced the material and seemed to catch the sun's rays whenever she moved.

Angeline lowered her gaze, her mind a flurry of wishes as she realized he was checking her out. "It is. The guy you saw me with yesterday. He's not just helping me with the surf lessons. He told me he could get my designs seen by some of the top surf brands."

Sam's heart dropped to his stomach with the reminder that she was free to date anyone she liked and this guy obviously had given her a few reasons why she should choose him. "Well, good luck with that," he said more formally than their earlier conversation. "Are you getting a lesson today?"

"No, Kai said he had something to do." She paused, but sensing a sudden awkwardness had developed, she spoke up. "Is something wrong?" Angeline somewhat hoped that he would give her a good reason to spend time with him, maybe even tell her that he could give her the lessons.

Instead, Sam plastered on a smile, aware of his duties -- where they started and unfortunately, where they ended. "No, I just think you should be extra careful when you surf with someone who is so...so..." Sam wanted to say "so obviously a tool and an ass," but he recovered and simply said, "someone who is so much more experienced. He may be a bit of a hot-dogger and go in when the surf is too high for you."

Angeline rolled her eyes, pride taking over her previous thoughts. "Thanks, but I can take care of myself and he has been an excellent teacher. I'm practically ready to go pro."

He smiled, forgetting all about the surfer for Angeline's humor melted his heart. "Okay, just be smart and safe."

She put her hand up to her forehead and gave Sam a cute salute. "I'm so embarrassed. I've just been going on and on. I don't know...you just seem familiar to me. Has anyone ever told you that you're a really good listener? I can't believe I don't even know your name. I'm Angeline, by the way."

"I'm Sam," he responded and extended his hand to her. "Listening comes with the job," Sam couldn't help but crack a smile. It seemed strange to introduce himself. She was right. He should seem familiar to her. After all, he had been watching over her for months now. It was like heaven on earth to be able to actually talk with her, to sit so close to her and hold her hand in his own. He hated the idea of releasing it when the heat of their touch poured through him.

With Sam's thumb making small circles over the back of her hand, her breath hitched and her voice grew smaller. "You make me feel comfortable, safe even."

The conversation had taken a turn. The connection he had long ago established as her guardian grew even stronger. He didn't know how he would ever fully release her to another man when that day came. Swallowing hard, he started by letting go of her hand.

"I wouldn't have expected a lifeguard to be such a good listener. After all, aren't most of the people you come into contact with drowning or something?"

A sudden chill hit the air and as the wind picked up a wave crashed with a thundering sound. Sam looked out toward the water with concern. As if the waves were playing a game of hide and seek, immediately the water became calm again. Evan was due to arrive soon, but even so, Sam felt he needed to get back to the tower in case the conditions grew more hazardous.

He shook off the uneasy thought that Angeline's words and the weather were related, and decided it was time that he should be on his way. No need to piss off the gods.

"I need to get back to my post."

"Oh, of course. It was really nice meeting you, Sam. Officially, that is." With that, Angeline picked up her board and headed toward the water.

"Hey, you're not going out now, are you?"

"Sure. The swells aren't too big and I won't get any better if I don't practice."

Sam looked out at the water, which remained calm. Still, he looked at Angeline with concern. Call it intuition or maybe superstition, but he couldn't shake the nervous feeling in the pit of his stomach that he shouldn't have spent so much time talking to the girl he loved, but was meant to be only an assignment.

"You be careful," he said with concern.

"I will. Thanks, Sam. Maybe I'll see you when I get out?"

In his mind he could swear he heard warning bells going off along with something else...as if a thousand angels were singing Hallelujah. He weighed the risks in his mind and finally, love won out. "I'll be here. Maybe we can grab a bite?"

Angeline smiled a wide, toothy grin that showed she really liked him too. "I'd love it. But I have to warn you...I'm pretty famished after hitting the water."

# # #

Chapter Ten

"How'd it go?" Evan asked when Sam got back to the lifeguard tower. "I saw you talking."

"We have a date." Sam grabbed the binoculars from where they hung and fixed his gaze on the water, scanning back and forth, not only for Angeline but for anyone else who may need help.

"Listen, Sam...as a lifeguard you can justify spending time with her here on the beach. But a date?"

"Alright, fine. Let's not call it a date. I'm going to eat after work, because that's what people do and she might happen to be there with me."

Evan raised his eyebrows, not buying any of it. "Eating."

"Yep, just chomping down on a big ol' something."

"Got it. But if I were you, I'd make sure this eating establishment doesn't have a candlelit table in the place."

# # #

After debating about where to eat, Sam joked that no restaurant could top his homemade tacos and Angeline dared him to prove it. Who was he to argue? He gave her directions to his small home in the midst of Topanga Canyon. It didn't take him long to clean up the bungalow since he didn't have many possessions -- one of the rules of angels. The home was comfortable and had all of the necessities without being overbearing or ostentatious.

Angeline arrived and surveyed the surroundings with an admiring glance. "This is magical," she said, looking out a floor to ceiling window that revealed a creek running through his backyard. "Look at all of these trees. And, it's so quiet here."

"It suits me," Sam admitted. "When one is this close to nature, you can't really find anything to get you down."

"You have a pretty remarkable life. The ocean by day and mountains at night." She stood facing him, close enough for him to pull her into an embrace. He wanted to, but he knew what it would lead to so he settled for taking her hand and leading her into the kitchen.

"Come on. Let's get you some food." The tacos were waiting on a heating tray and the table was laid, but Sam just shook his head.

"Something wrong?"

In his mind, Sam had gone through all the scenarios. He knew what getting close to Angeline could do to him. He knew that he had vowed to let her go and just watch her from afar. But hadn't he already messed up that promise? She was here in his house and the proximity to her was driving him mad. "Grab a plate, fill it with as many tacos as you can possibly consume and follow me."

She laughed, but did as she was instructed. Sam led her to the small porch that ran along the entire back of the house. A large oak tree was situated in the middle of the yard, but through its branches one could still admire the moonlight and stars. They took their places next to each other on a swinging bench made just for two. Its plush cushions caused them to sink into each other, but neither made any attempt to put distance between them.

A small tin can filled with kerosene wax sat on a makeshift table, actually an old trunk from a bygone era. Sam lit it and the space was bathed in a romantic glow.

"This place, your home...it's so peaceful. And these tacos are just as heavenly." Angeline had nearly finished off one already.

"I marinate the chicken in cilantro and serrano chiles before cooking it. My secret," Sam said in a conspiratorial tone before pouring her another glass of wine and took a sip from his own glass. He recalled Evan's comment about candlelight and thought that certainly a tin can couldn't constitute romance.

"Pretty romantic," Angeline whispered to him, causing Sam to inadvertently look skyward. When nothing happened, no lightening or sudden downpour, he took it as a sign that he hadn't totally overstepped his guardian angel boundaries. It's just dinner, he rationalized. But then Angeline put her plate down on the porch and settled in closer to Sam, inspiring him to put his arm around her.

Angels don't normally drink wine and the effects were already getting to him. The alcohol, coupled with Angeline's perfume, were an intoxicating combination. He inhaled the scent of her and then without thinking, brought his lips to the top of her head. It was such a gentle kiss, not sexual but utterly caring and it showed just how much he felt for her.

"You're a great guy, Sam."

His head was now swimming from the wine and his answer came out without thinking. "I've learned a few things up there."

Angeline looked up at him confused. "Up there?"

"I mean, before I lived here, I was stationed a bit further north. Just watch the stars," he said softly, diverting her attention. "There's usually a shooting one from time to time. They say every shooting star is an angel falling in love."

He lifted the lid on a large wicker basket that sat next to their seat and retrieved a couple of blankets. Throwing one over their shoulders and another over their legs, Sam held Angeline in comfortable silence.

# # #

Chapter Eleven

"Check it out," Sam said to Evan, indicating his not-so-favorite surfer in the parking lot.

"For a surfer he sure spends a lot of time in the parking lot," Evan noted.

"Last night Angeline said he wouldn't be here today."

Evan nodded, then broached the subject. "So is she quitting her lessons?"

Sam shook his head. "She's not quitting, but she has no intention of dating him, so that's something."

"Dangerous ground," Evan warned.

Not wanting to continue the conversation, Sam started to head in the direction of the surfer. "Seems a little fishy, if you ask me. I'm gonna check it out. After all, he's still standing on our jurisdiction."

In spite of heading away from the water, Sam still grabbed the handheld life preserver. It was required for lifeguards to carry it at all times in case they suddenly had to handle a rescue. But besides that prerequisite reason, Sam had found that the sturdy plastic came in handy when a fight broke out. With this guy, he wasn't about to take any chances.

He approached and immediately noticed the surfer's jittery stance. He was in perpetual movement as was the guy he stood with. When Sam got close enough, he could see his pupils were dilated.

"Shouldn't you be back in your hut?"

"Not when duty calls out here," Sam said evenly.

"And what sort of duty is that?" the mangy guy that stood with the surfer asked with an edge to his voice. "We're not doing nothin'."

Sam noted that his arms were covered in track marks indicative of a heroine addict.

He recalled the needle that he found buried in the kelp.

"That's a double negative, which means you're actually up to something. Why don't you get back in your van and I'll pretend I didn't see anything. You can drive away and I won't call the authorities, that is, as long as you never return."

The surfer got right in Sam's face so he could smell the mixture of pot and whiskey on his breath. "I got a problem with that lifeguard. This is my beach. My office. And I'll damn well do my business here, and you got nothing on me."

"Kai, let's get outta here. Smells like pig - - saltwater pig," the guy standing with the surfer said, gesturing to Sam. The two got into the van and drove off, but they left Sam with the distinct feeling that the discarded needles originated from Kai. He just had to prove it.

# # #

Chapter Twelve

There was something about the cyclical ways of the beach that calmed Sam. The day would start with a deserted beach and after the last of the sun worshippers and frisbee throwers had left, the sun would begin its slow descent giving way once again to an unencumbered stretch of white sand. As he saw the last of the families leave, he surveyed the stretch of beach and saw that only a few diehards were still in the water.

Most were experienced surfers. Sam recognized a few as being part of Kai's crew. Among them was Angeline, looking small and a bit lost, but for whatever reason she continued to stay out.

Looking out at the water, Sam noticed that the swells were picking up as the day was growing tired.

"You know, sometimes people are having so much fun they don't always know when to come in," Evan commented.

"She's not ready for these swells and those yahoos aren't paying her any notice," Sam added with growing concern, knowing where Evan's thoughts lay. "I think this qualifies as guardian angel territory. You mind covering?"

"It's nearly closing time. I've got this. You go look after your girl."

# # #

Sam swam easily out to where Angeline was on her board and greeted her with a friendly wave.

"You're off duty?"

Sam smiled inwardly, knowing that he was never really off duty, but nonetheless, responded with his usual easy mannerism.

"That I am. Thought I'd catch a wave before I go home...but I think they're getting too big."

Indeed the pull of the ocean was separating him from Angeline even as they spoke. She was drifting farther away and he found he had to yell to communicate. Angeline squinted her eyes at him and gave him a knowing look. "Is that a nice way of you actually telling me that I'm too much of a newbie to be out here now?"

Sam didn't respond directly, but decided diplomacy was in order. "I promise the ocean will be here tomorrow."

Angeline laughed and from her vantage point about twelve feet beyond where Sam was floating on his board, decided he was right. "Okay, one last ride and I'll call it a day."

The ocean was forming what the locals called a perfect A-frame, a barreling surf with a cross-section that forms an A. For an experienced surfer, it was heaven, but for someone of Angeline's skill level, it could be dangerous. She noted the wave as it started to form behind her and positioned herself to go for it, but her ascent onto the board was a couple seconds late and she inadvertently cut off one of Kai's guys.

Not taking kindly to a new surfer, let alone a woman taking his wave, the renegade surfer clipped across her board, causing her to lose balance right in the midst of the barrel. She flipped over hard, her board skyrocketing upwards and then crashing down on top of her, pinning her under the water for a few agonizing and terrifying seconds. Had Sam not been there to see it and immediately get her up, the next waves would have pummeled her.

Holding Angeline with one arm, Sam steadied her board with the other and easily pulled her onto it. His strong pectoral muscles and biceps flexed and cued his supernatural abilities to kick in, lending him a strength that was unparalleled.

"What the hell, Barney?" the renegade surfer had come back for another ride and sent a searing look along with the disparaging moniker in Angeline's direction.

Sam had been around the surf culture long enough to pick up on the lingo as well as the attitude. "Hey, don't go getting all aggro out here," he said, referring to the aggressive behavior.

The surfer stared at him as if he wasn't even speaking English. That's when Sam noticed his pupils and how they were oddly large. As if realizing that even in the water Sam held the authority to haul him onto shore and send him packing, the surfer started to paddle away, preparing to charge another round of waves.

"You're not worth my time, lifeguard!" he yelled back, now feeling cocky as he was surrounded by three other surfers. "And you, Barney...if you're not with Kai, you're not meant to be here. Stick with the ankle busters," he said referring to the small waves.

Angeline was noticeably shook up, both by her wipeout and the aggression of the other surfer. Sam brushed a strand of hair out of her eyes and lifted her chin up so they were eye to eye. "Don't let him get to you. I'll get you back to shore now."

They were floating in a precarious place, neither in position to catch a wave nor farther back, but rather what the surfers referred to as caught inside. The positioning was dangerous and the waves were coming one on top of the next, throwing Angeline's usual confidence for a loop.

"Sam, I don't think I can get in."

"Yes, you can."

"I'm scared," she admitted, and clung to her board with two hands.

"You have to listen to me and trust me. You're safe with me. Do you believe me?" Sam spoke firmly, but calmly. He had been trained for this and Angeline was seeing him in a professional light. Kai and his crew were cocky surfers, developing their skills from taking big risks both with their lives and others. Sam, on the other hand, had a calming presence and an athlete's precision. She trusted him and in answer to his question, she gave an affirming nod.

Standing behind Angeline, Sam guided the board across the barrel of the wave. Riding with expert skill and a little help from above, which he used to navigate his own board back to shore, Sam maintained a comforting, but appropriate hold on

Angeline's waist, steadying her until they reached the shoreline.

"How can I ever thank you?"

Without considering whether she was still into Kai or not, and certainly not thinking of the ramifications from above, he responded quickly and with assurance. "Let's go to dinner. A proper date this time. Don't think," he said as much in warning to himself as her. "Let's just do it. Right now."

# # #

Chapter Thirteen

"I can't go to dinner looking like this." She was wearing a beach cover-up over her bikini and to Sam, she looked beautiful. But he noticed that she was shivering slightly so he attended to her needs by giving her his lifeguard's jacket and wrapping a blanket over her shoulders as he walked her to his car.

"I'll bring you back tomorrow for your car. You shouldn't drive after all that."

Angeline raised her eyebrows, the question on her face becoming apparent.

"Don't worry. I'm going to drive you to your house where you can get warm and changed."

She seemed to weigh up what he was saying until finally, he stated the fear that was on his mind. "Unless you don't want to go out..."

"No!" she exclaimed. "It's not that, at all. I just would rather you make dinner for me again. Can we stay in?"

He couldn't stop the huge smile that emerged on his face. "Definitely."

"But can you cook at my place? I'm kind of tired from everything."

Sam zipped up the jacket he had given her so it was fastened just under her neck. "I can do that."

Angeline bit her lower lip and looked at him as if she wondered just what else he was capable of doing. "So, you can really cook, huh?"

Sam nodded with confidence. "Like an angel."

"Hmm, that I'll have to see because let me tell you...there are mighty slim pickins at my house," she teased, putting on a country bumpkin accent.

"All I need are a few basics. I assure you we'll be fine," he said as he opened the passenger door to his car.

Angeline slid in, but before Sam closed the door, she added, "I feel more than fine already. Thank you, Sam."

# # #

Two big Adirondack chairs sat on the lawn just in front of Angeline's home, inviting visitors to come and sit awhile. The small, craftsman style home featured a bright red door with a myriad of potted plants on either side.

As Angeline tried unsuccessfully to unlock the door, Sam took the keys from her shaking hand. "Here, let me help," he said, easily pushing back the door and revealing the sitting room, which was open and homey with dark wood paneled floors, a small sofa, and a over-sized chair that he couldn't help thinking would be a cozy place for him to take her onto his lap. "You go find something dry and warm to put on and I'll get dinner started."

"Good luck with that," she said, while being greeted by Buchanon, her Yorkshire Terrier. "Hi sweetie. You ready for din-din?" She started down the hallway toward the kitchen with her dog in her arms and Sam at her heels.

"How old is he?"

"Just two. Still a pup. So, I'm going to feed him and then take your advice."

"I can feed him, if you like. You should really get in a warm bath."

Angeline eyed him, but didn't answer immediately. The electricity between them was palpable.

Sam felt it too. The minute he made the comment about the bath, his thoughts went to her being there and how much he would like to join her. It seemed she read his mind as he could see her taking in his strong physique, her eyes moving over his body.

"Go on," he said, ushering her away. He knew if she didn't leave for the other room now, dinner may never get prepared.

"Okay. One scoop of kibble for Buchanon and a quarter can of dog food. Everything's in the pantry."

"You got it." He extended his hands to her and took the dog out of her arms, wrinkling his nose a bit at the smell of him.

"Sorry. He's a little dirty. I was supposed to wash him today."

"It's nothing." He smiled and carried the dog into the kitchen, taking his time to first admire black and white photos that hung on the walls depicting surfers catching remarkable waves. Although the photos were spectacular, they left him with a bad taste as he was reminded of Kai. Not wanting to dwell on anything unpleasant, Sam pursued the task at hand: feed the dog and then create dinner out of what Angeline warned would be sparse findings.

She wasn't joking. When Sam opened the refrigerator, he found a take-out container with the remains of an enchilada, a couple of yogurts, some eggs and cheese, and a head of lettuce. A peak into the freezer revealed that there wasn't a chicken breast nor a veggie patty to be found. But Sam was resourceful and immediately got to work.

# # #

At the insistence of Sam, Angeline had taken up residence on the couch, curled up under a blanket that he insisted putting over her when she emerged from her bath wearing a breezy dress.

"Are you warm enough?" he called from the kitchen where he was still putting the final touches on dinner.

"I'm fine, really. Except, it smells too good to stay here any longer." She tiptoed into the kitchen and when he gave her a mock scowl, she only added. "My stomach's growling. I have to know what smells so good. I don't think my house has ever experienced any real cooking going on inside of it."

He moved a chair back from the table and indicated she should take a seat. "Cheese souffle and your timing is perfect. I think it's ready." Grabbing a pair of oven mitts, he retrieved a casserole dish from the oven that was brimming to the top with a pale yellow mixture that looked to be light as air.

"You made this from my kitchen?" Angeline asked in disbelief. "Are you sure you didn't order in from a restaurant when I wasn't paying attention?"

"All you need are a few eggs, cheese, milk, flour and salt."

"Milk?"

"I found some powdered milk in the cupboard so I whipped that up to get started. I think I'm going to have to teach you about staple items." He smiled, feeling completely at home in being able to tease her because of the way she looked back at him. "Go on, taste it."

Angeline did as she was told and immediately exclaimed, "Oh my goodness. Sooo yummy!" With her eyes closed, she savored the taste.

Seated right next to her, Sam watched her in awe. She was beautiful, not just physically, but within her heart as well. He had loved her from the moment he was first assigned to watch over her. He leaned in closer to brush a hair away from her face.

Close enough, in fact, that he could have kissed her.

He imagined what it would be like to touch his lips to hers. A kiss between them would be warm and soft with the promise of the love he felt for her. He placed the strand of hair behind her ear and then brought his hand up to caress her cheek.

She opened her eyes and stared at him wide-eyed, quite aware of his proximity and yet making no move to put distance between them. In fact, her breath hitched, her mouth parted, she re-closed her eyes and waited in giddy anticipation of what might come.

But he couldn't get involved. Even though it was merely a kiss he had imagined, a kiss held such hope.

"Can I get you some more?" he asked, breaking the moment.

"Sure." The disappointment in her voice was noticeable. Sam knew that she must be totally confused. How many guys wouldn't make a move? As if to reassure him that it would be acceptable to her if he did, she added in a husky voice, "I can't wait to have more."

What the hell was he thinking? He was ready to throw the dishes on the floor and lie her down on top of the table. "Yeah, I'd like more too," he said, his voice low and his eyes holding hers a bit longer than was necessary.

They spoke in double entendres and Sam knew it wasn't wise to lead her on, but he couldn't help it. He desperately wanted her. His resolve was faltering with every glance she sent him.

They turned their attention to the meal and ate in comfortable silence, enjoying the food too much to bother with words. And when they were finished, Angeline placed the dishes in the dishwasher and looked around the kitchen for the bowls and utensils that Sam must have used to make the souffle.

It was then that she realized that not a dirty dish was in sight. In fact, the counters even appeared cleaner than when she had left that morning. The toaster was completely void of its usual crumbs. The metal refrigerator door gleamed.

"You are heaven sent," she said to Sam. "The only thing left to be cleaned is Buchanon," she joked.

Dinner was over, but he didn't want to leave. He would do anything to stay with her just a bit longer...including wash the dog. "Let's do it."

"Seriously? He gets even smellier when he's wet. You would really help me?"

"I'm game." He picked up Buchanon and followed Angeline to the utility porch adjoining her kitchen where she reached into high cupboards to retrieve the shampoo. As she stood on her tiptoes and extended her arm above her head, the dress she wore rose up to reveal the top of her thighs. As Sam watched her, thoughts that were decidedly un-angelic flitted through his mind. He looked at the small dog in his arms and mouthed "thank you."

# # #

Chapter Fourteen

Angeline placed Buchanon in the sink and turned on the water, testing the temperature before holding the nozzle over him. "He's actually pretty good. He doesn't seem to mind the water." As if to rectify this falsehood, the little dog shook himself from head to tail. "Usually," she corrected and continued directing the water over him.

When Buchanon was sufficiently drenched, Sam reached for the shampoo bottle and poured a small capful onto Buchanon's back. While bathing the dog, they stood next to each other, heat radiating off their bodies and their hands brushing against each other as they massaged shampoo into the dog's fur. As if sensing the tension, Buchanon once again shook himself, spraying a substantial amount of water all over Angeline.

"Ugh...Buchanon, how could you?" She held up her arms revealing that the Dolman sleeves of her dress were soaked. She reacted without thinking, pulling the dress over her head. Realizing where her instincts had taken her, she simply explained, "Well, it's practically like a bathing suit and it's not like you haven't seen me in one of those before."

But this wasn't a bathing suit. Below her dress was a black lace bra and pantie set. As if only now realizing the full effect she had on Sam, she met his gaze, but couldn't find words. He stared at her hungrily, taking in her ample breasts, small waist, and the curve of her hips.

"The hell with it." He reached for her, pulling her close to him. His mouth covered hers hard and then moved down her neck and over the curve of her breast that extended above her bra.

"Buchanon," she whispered breathlessly. "He's all soapy."

Sam begrudgingly pulled himself away and noticed that she had kept a hand on the dog the entire time, ensuring that he didn't jump out of the sink. If Sam didn't know better, the little Terrier seemed to laugh at him, its mouth pulled back in a funny expression.

"Got soap in your mouth?" he muttered.

"I guess we should finish washing him up," Angeline hedged.

Sam nodded once and then took a deep, cleansing breath. He wondered to himself if this were another example of God working in mysterious ways.

# # #

Angeline had finished washing up Buchanon. In truth, Sam was of no help from the minute she had taken off her wet clothes. No way was what she was wearing anything like a bathing suit. She stood before him in what had to be the sexiest silk lingerie he could imagine. Although Sam found her bathing suit designs to be both flattering and stylish, this was better. Much better.

He stood back, putting a bit of space between them because he just couldn't be this close and not touch her. He couldn't keep his eyes off her and the sight of her was too arousing for him to not be affected. When she lifted Buchanon out of the sink and bent down to place him on the floor, she looked up to see his erection straining against his pants.

Her eyes opened wide with the knowledge of how well-endowed he was. "Oh God. You make me want to do...everything. Now."

She reached her hand up to him and he pulled her to her feet and into his arms. Their hands still entwined, Angeline led Sam to the sitting room and the couch. The moment she kissed him, a chill traveled his spine. If one were a romantic they would say it was electric. Sam was just that sort of romantic, but he was also a realist and knew that the spark wasn't only the excitement of touching Angeline, it was literally a jolt sent from above -- a warning that he should be leaving.

Whispering against her mouth he said, "You had a scare today."

Her tongue lapped against his lower lip, his mouth nibbled her ear. "I'm safe now," she murmured.

"You should probably get some rest. I should go."

It wasn't an empty sentiment. Sam had every intention of leaving -- of pleasing the power above. Until Angeline whispered seductively. "I think you should stay."

# # #

Chapter Fifteen

Soft music played and candles flickered on the coffee table. The setting was perfect for romance and with Angeline leaning into him, Sam couldn't think of anything he would rather do than continue to kiss her, except maybe to hold her for the rest of time.

As his mouth traveled over hers, his mind told him that he had to get control of this situation. If God were staring down at him...well, he just couldn't imagine what type of ramifications there would be for holding Angeline in her current state of undress. "Damn...," he muttered realizing that he shouldn't have reminded himself of that fact.

"Hmm?" she murmured.

"Nothing. Just that, you are so damn beautiful."

He could feel her smile under his lips. Wasn't making her happy the reason for his existence? He would tell her one more truth and then he would leave. He made a silent promise to God.

"Your skin is so soft," he said running his hand over her back, pulling her even closer to him in what he believed to be a goodbye hug. Under his breath he whispered, "I wish I could do this forever."

But whereas Sam intended to leave, Angeline had other ideas. "Maybe if I do this, you will try and do it forever." She reached for his hand and placed it on her breast, then unhooked her bra in one fast move.

"Oh Angeline." Not exactly the result he intended, but he was helpless to argue. He bent his head to her breast and took her nipple into his mouth, lightly caressing the bud with his tongue, flicking small circles over it until hard peaks formed. She moaned and threw her head back, pulling his mouth harder onto her.

"Hell. I'm done for..." Sam acknowledged and with one easy move, he pulled Angeline onto his lap where his erection nestled between her legs.

"I feel underdressed," she hinted with a glint in her eye.

He wanted nothing more than to rid himself of the clothes that confined him and become one with Angeline. But the love and desire he felt battled with the oath he had taken.

If he accommodated what she was suggesting there would be no turning back.

A sudden wind storm caused a branch on a tree outside to snap and fall to the ground with a large bang, making both of them jump.

"Weird. That just came out of nowhere," Angeline said, turning toward the window.

But Sam suspected it wasn't as random as she believed. It served to break the moment between them and he knew that he was nearing the point where desire could no longer be curbed. It was time he was on his way.

Concentrating on Angeline, he forced the events of the day to bring sleep to her. Within seconds, fatigue affected her and she yawned. His tactics worked in spite of his desire to the contrary.

She covered her mouth as another yawn escaped her. "I'm so sorry."

"Come here," he said and raised his arm for her to cozy up next to him. She placed her head on his shoulder, closed her eyes and slumber took her immediately. Sam carried her to her room and placed her under the covers before retreating back down the hall and leaving for the night.

As he closed her front door, he sighed wistfully. To have stayed with her would have been heaven, but as if God were still watching and ensuring he didn't try anything, the wind blew again. Sam gave one final glance behind him before leaving the small cottage and making his way to his car and into the night.

# # #

Chapter Sixteen

The following day was a typically glorious one in Malibu. The sun shone on the water making it glisten. But Sam's mood contrasted severely with the brightness of the day. Evan noted Sam's quiet demeanor and questioned him about it.

"Something happen last night?"

Sam shook his head in the negative, but remained tight-lipped.

Evan may have been easy-going, but he was still Sam's senior when it came to setting an example of obeying the guardian angel bylaws. He made the decision that he'd rather be labeled a stick in the mud than see his friend get in trouble. Deciding to forgo his usual easy-going nonchalance, he persevered in getting the truth out of Sam.

"I thought you were dropping Angeline at home after that run-in with the wave and then leaving for a quiet evening alone. How'd that go?"

"We had a slight change of plans," Sam admitted, but didn't offer more.

Evan nodded his head, but wore an expression that he wasn't buying any of it. "As in you didn't leave right away change of plans?"

Sam turned to face him. "What? Are you the Angel Police now? How'd you know?"

"Your face shows an odd mix of guilt and puppy dog love. Tell me nothing happened."

"Of course not. Who do you think I am? One of the guys down there?" Sam motioned southward. He paused as if contemplating just how close he came and finally admitted, "I just don't know how long my resolve will hold."

"We're about to find out." Evan motioned behind Sam to where Angeline was navigating the wooden stairs leading away from the parking lot. She wore another halter style bikini, this one in pale pink with two green palm tree leaves placed in a most strategic position and one more that graced the front of her bikini bottom.

"God help me," Sam muttered before waving his morning hello to Angeline.

When she reached the lifeguard tower, he saw that she was carrying a small loaf-shaped object wrapped in tin foil. "This is for you. Just something to help you get through the day without any hunger pangs. It's a chocolate chip banana bread. My grandmother's recipe, and just about the best thing in the world. It's also the only thing that I really know how to bake."

Sam took it and peaked underneath the foil. "It smells amazing. You didn't have to do this. When did you even have time? It's bright and early and you were out like a light last night."

"I woke up early to bake it. It's my way of saying thank you for making me that delicious dinner as well as apologizing for falling asleep on you."

Sam felt a momentary tinge of guilt in letting her think that she had been the one to fall asleep when in reality it was all his doing. Besides, his reasoning for making her sleep wasn't anywhere close to being noble.

As if sensing the turmoil that his friend was going through, Evan jumped in. "Heck, I feel like falling asleep when Sam talks to me as well."

Angeline laughed in spite of attempts to restrain herself. "Rain check?" she asked Sam, when she had recovered.

"Definitely. Let's do that soon."

Before Angeline could respond, an unwanted voice took her place. "Do what lifeguard?"

Surfer. Asshole. No matter what moniker Sam put on him, the fact remained the same. His voice was as grating as the first time Sam had heard it. As if validating that fact, Sam cringed as Kai continued, "You 'bout ready, sweetheart?"

No way. Sam knew his face must have looked as if he were about ready to take a swing at the guy. He steadied himself and jumped onto the tower's platform before turning a steely expression toward the water. Angeline lightly touched his leg that dangled over the edge of the platform above her. She leaned closer and kept her voice low.

"Sam, it's not what you think. I agreed to this last lesson before...before last night. And, Kai's sponsor is going to be here today. He's looking at some of my designs."

"It's fine," Sam responded stiffly. "You do what you need to. I need to get to work."

"Sure," she said sadly. "About that rain check?"

"Soon," he said, but his tone was non-committal.

"You sound mad," she pressed.

"You don't owe me any sort of explanation. It was just dinner; it didn't mean anything."

"Yeah. That's what I thought." She glared at Sam and he knew he deserved it, but he never expected what she would do next. The old phrase, "Hell hath no fury like a woman scorned" bore into his mind as he watched in disappointment as Angeline pivoted towards Kai and turned up the charm.

"I've been looking forward to this," she said leaning in close enough for him to wrap an arm around her waist. She stared up at Kai and smiled sweetly. Any man would have reacted and Kai was no exception. He wrapped his arm around Angeline's waist and pulled her in for a kiss. Although Angeline broke it off almost as soon as it started, she had after all been the one to instigate it.

Kai smirked at Sam before he grabbed Angeline's board with one arm and her hand with his other. As Sam watched her walk away, he felt as if a piece of his heart left with her as well.

# # #

Chapter Seventeen

Angeline tried to brighten her mood in spite of feeling torn about leaving Sam.

"You're gonna shine for me, right? This guy is the big time. If he likes your designs, he can turn you into the next big surf brand." He put an arm around Angeline and whispered in her ear. "You're too beautiful to wear a frown."

"That's sweet," Angeline replied, but felt herself recoil from his touch.

"Hey, don't forget who got you here. There he is," he motioned up the beach to where another guy stood watching the waves with his board.

"That's him?" Angeline was surprised that the big merchandiser they were meeting appeared to be an ordinary surfer.

"Just keeping it real. You can't be relatable to the surf crowd if you sit behind a desk wearing a suit. That goes for you, too, which is why you're learning to surf."

They reached the other surfer and Kai made the introductions. "Howard, I'd like you to meet Angeline, an amazing clothing designer specializing in surf wear and my protege where surfing is concerned."

He held out his hand to Angeline and after looking her over, winked at Kai as if they shared an inside story. "Call me Hoagie. Nice suit, by the way. One of your designs?"

"Yes, thank you. I brought some sketches for you to see," she said pulling her backpack off.

He waved his hand in dismissal. "In a bit. I need a wake-up first. Didn't have time for coffee this morning," he said by way of explanation as he pulled a baggie of white powder out of his own pack. "Kai, you want in?"

"Hell, yeah."

Howard slid his hand across his board, cleaning away the sand, before removing the contents of the baggie along with a razor blade. He went to work chopping up the powder even finer than it already was, rolled up a piece of paper and then handed it to Kai.

Kai snorted a fat line before knocking his head back and giving a little victory yelp. "Oh yeah, that's good shit. Here," he said handing the paper back to Howard.

"Does your girl want some?" he asked, eyeballing Angeline as if he were trying to figure her out.

"Oh, I'm not his girl," Angeline answered instinctively only to be received by an ugly glare from Kai.

"Spunky. I like that," Howard joked. "Kai, you know I consider this place to be my playground," he said motioning to the vast expanse of ocean.

Kai was already feeling the effects of the cocaine. "And a wonderful playground it is."

"So, don't forget your school house lessons. Share! I know you don't show up here without your product."

"You know it!" Kai jumped about like a runner preparing for a sprint. He fluttered his hands in preparation for the next unsavory activity and then to Angeline's horror, produced a hypodermic needle from a pocket in his board shorts.

"There it is. Give me some of that," Howard rubbed his hands together and then extended his forearm toward Kai. "Ahh, would you look at that wave! I'll be right back," he said, taking off toward the ocean at a vigorous run before the deed could be completed.

Angeline looked toward the lifeguard tower, wishing that it was time for Sam to take a patrol of the beach. She was too far away to determine if he had his binoculars trained on them, but even if he had, Kai was crouched in a ball, avoiding any onlooker stares.

Her repulsion grew as she watched him shoot the needle into his vein. The effects were a momentary lull before he looked out at the ocean and decided in his messed up mind that surfing was actually a good idea.

"You're not going out there now, are you?" Angeline asked Kai in disbelief.

"Ahh, you do care," he said and pulled her in for a hug. He was still holding the needle and Angeline moved carefully out of his grip for fear of being stabbed by it. With a mixture of relief and anger, she watched as he tossed it onto the sand.

"You can't leave that there. Someone might step on it."

"So do whatever you want with it and then grab your board," Kai hissed, not liking her demanding tone. "And stop acting like an uppity-goody-two-shoes. You need to relax if you're going to get Hoagie to trust you and want to work with you. Right now you seem like a total narc." He grabbed his board and walked toward the ocean without waiting for an answer.

Angeline fumed as she watched him leave, and then turning once more toward the lifeguard tower, she knew what she had to do. The plastic baggie that had contained the cocaine was discarded on the sand, littering the beach along with the needle. She watched as it fluttered on the wind, moving in circles up the sand. Quickly, she stepped on the bag to stop it and then bent to pick it up, touching just a corner of it. Using a rock, she pushed the needle into the bag, sealed it up and then hid it in her backpack.

Kai had just finished a long run as the waves were big, but he was heading back onto the shore when she put her backpack on her beach towel and went to sit down.

"Don't get comfortable. You're up," he announced while shaking his long hair like a dog emerging from the water.

"What do you mean?"

"Get in the water." Kai's voice had taken on an angry tone.

"Kai, I can't. The waves are too big." Angeline knew the minute she uttered her fear that it would go unheard. The drugs were clearly impairing his judgement. *Please Sam*...she silently prayed. *Take your patrol. Now.*

"You are a commodity to me. So come on." Kai pointed toward her board, and begrudgingly Angeline obeyed.

# # #

Chapter Eighteen

Sam kept his binoculars trained on Angeline, not wanting to take his eyes off her while at the same time hating what he was seeing.

"Sam, you need to watch the entire beach," Evan reminded him.

Sam handed the binoculars over. "Here. I'm having trouble focusing on anything left of over there." He pointed to where Angeline was surfing.

Evan took the binoculars and offered his sage advice. "You know, as her guardian angel you need to tune into more than just what you see. It's about instinct as well."

"If every one of these grains of sand was shouting for me to go get her that still would be a softer voice than the one in my head." Sam raked his hand through his blond hair and pressed his lips into a tight grimace.

"What do you mean?" Evan asked cautiously.

"I mean it's like she's shouting at me to come and get her. I always have her on my mind, but this is insane. It's like my entire body is on edge with worry."

"Just go. Now!"

Sam didn't have to be told twice. He grabbed his lifeguard's buoy and jumped from the platform, easily landing on the sand below. Ripping off his red jacket he took off towards the shore at a run, attracting the attention of many beach-goers who now stood up wondering if a rescue was in progress.

It didn't take Sam long to run the quarter-mile down the beach to where Angeline was surfing. He looked out at the water and saw her lying on her stomach on her board. She was farther out than he felt was comfortable for her, but the only saving grace was that the waves weren't breaking too hard at that distance.

When Kai rode one into shore, Sam was there to meet him.

"Whacha want guard?" he slurred.

Sam could see immediately that his eyes were glassy and his face had an odd pallor to it. "It's getting rough out there. Even you have to know that she's not ready for these waves."

"I've got this lifeguard. It's what I do," he stated with all the cockiness of a bull rider, and then turned to go out again, but stumbled and fell, landing face first in the water. He pulled himself upright, spluttering and spitting in a manner that disgusted Sam, but still he carried on walking back out into the water.

"You're so high, you can't even look after yourself, let alone her. What are you doing?"

Kai returned to the water, but Sam followed suit, easily catching up to him with strong strokes. Enjoying his ability to get under Sam's skin, Kai laughed and then threw his hand into the water like a spoiled child, causing a small wave to hit Sam square in the face. Turning, the surfer narrowed his eyes and then spoke slowly, deliberately mocking him. "You wanna know what I'm doing? I'm surfing with my girl. My very hot and sexy girl. No need for you to be here."

"Your girl?"

"Yep."

Sam didn't respond. He knew that Kai was trash, but where Angeline was concerned at least he was alive, a regular man whom she could date if she wanted. No matter how much he disliked the situation, he had to let it play itself out. It didn't make his circumstance any easier to bear, but he started to turn away, resolved that he had no choice.

But then that niggling tingling feeling hit his gut again. He looked out to where Angeline still floated on her board. She was a bit closer in and he could now see that she looked positively nervous, clinging to the board as if the very idea of trying to stand up was ludicrous.

Maybe a regular guy isn't what she needs, he reasoned. Maybe being a guardian angel meant intervening. *I'll give him one*

last chance. If he's cool, I walk away. If he's
an insensitive jerk...well...

"Just be careful. The waves are picking up. She's not used to being on a board alone." As if to emphasize Sam's point, a wave came crashing down just a few feet from where they were. Both men shook it off and then looked out to Angeline.

"You see? No biggie." Kai maneuvered from lying on his stomach to straddling his board in a seated position. "Anyway, she's not alone. I'm right there with her. Oh and tonight, I'll do one better. Reel her in and show her what I've got."

As if his words weren't vulgar enough, he pumped his crotch into the surf board to demonstrate just what he had in mind. Sam was ready to pummel Kai, but he had no real justification for doing so. He knew Kai was high, but without physical proof that he partook in any drugs on his beach, Sam was unable to make a restraining arrest against him.

Although Kai goaded him on verbally, he hadn't taken any aggressive action against

Sam. His hands were tied and any hopes of calling in the authorities dissipated like sand through his fingers. He was sorting through the possibilities of how to get Kai off his beach when Angeline paddled over.

"Ahh, my girl's here," Kai said, gilding the lily of Sam's ire.

Ignoring him, Sam turned to Angeline. "The swells are going to rise with the oncoming offshore winds. It's not advisable to stay out any longer."

Angeline looked out to the ocean. Its light blue color from earlier in the day had turned dark and menacing with the waves growing stronger by the minute. There were still plenty of surfers in the water, but they had the combination of experience, arrogance and maybe a bit of a death wish as they hot dogged the waves, egging each other on and accepting challenges to see who could ride the longest and hardest. Angeline had no desire to stay in the water, but her pride won out.

"Thanks for your concern," she said cooly. "I'll be fine."

Sam had every right to be angry, but he wasn't. He was her guardian angel and he had taken an oath to protect her. He had learned a few things since becoming an angel and one of them was that God indeed worked in mysterious ways. He had to trust that things would work out as they were supposed to.

"Angeline," he called out. She turned and looked at him, but her expression remained stoney. "I'll be here for you," he added.

Although she didn't abandon her surfing session, she did appear as if her heart was starting to win out over her pride. Finally, she relented just a bit and mouthed a thank you to Sam, before Howard called her over and reluctantly, her career goals influenced her common sense.

# # #

Chapter Nineteen

Howard liked what he saw in Angeline. She seemed like a sweet girl and after learning that she had designed her bikini herself, it was obvious that she had talent as well. What she saw in Kai was beyond him. She was definitely out of his league. He decided to do right by her and promised to get her designs shown. But for now, he had some business to attend to with Kai.

"I know your designs are epic. Let's see how the surfing is coming along. You go for a run while I talk business with Kai."

Kai pulled his board next to Angeline's and placed his arm around her back, then addressed Sam, who was still staying close by. "Beat it, guard. We're fine here."

Angeline's eyes met Sam's, and when Kai leaned toward her, Sam continued to watch. He didn't want to see the display, but was unable to tear his eyes away. Yet, he was quickly vindicated when Angeline turned at precisely the right moment to offer Kai her cheek before paddling away.

You show him, Angel. Sam gave a satisfied nod and headed back to shore. Once there, he ran back to the lifeguard platform to get his hands on those binoculars and maintain an eye on her. He couldn't stay in Kai's midst, but there was no stopping him from doing his angel duties. He decided right then and there that Angeline was more than an assignment and worth any risk to his own status on Earth.

# # #

It might have been the fact that Angeline had been practicing surfing for hours on end. Perhaps it was simply a miracle...an angel watching over her. Whatever the case, she caught a wave and rode it into shore like an expert.

"You've got a winner with that girl. Triple threat. She's got the design skills; she fits in with the surf culture; and, she's got a lot of sexy going on. I wouldn't mind getting down with that."

Kai was just starting to come off his high, but he forced a laugh and gave Howard a high five. It was a time when tempers tended to flair unless put at ease and Kai was well aware of this fact. He was ready to call it a day and get back to his van where he had a joint waiting. He wasn't about to admit that Sam was right about the waves getting too rough. He was just thinking he needed something to hit the spot after the intense high of his cocaine morphine cocktail.

"Hey Hoagie!" he called out. "Ready to adios this beach?"

Howard paddled over, leaving Angeline behind. "Yeah, I'm getting ready to haul. But I've been thinking...I know you want me to manufacture one of her designs and include it in my fall catalog. You would get a pretty hefty commission for finding her, but I need something too..." He winked his eye and wiggled his tongue back and forth over his upper teeth.

Kai laughed out loud. "Oh yeah. I hear you. Wouldn't that be something. But she's cold as ice, man."

Howard looked out at Angeline, his thoughts unreadable. Finally, he turned back to Kai more serious than before. "That's too bad. Maybe you can thaw her out. I would've liked some threesome action."

Kai squinted his eyes, feeling a massive headache coming on. "I hear you, but that ain't gonna happen."

"Okay, I'm cool...just as long as you make up for it. Otherwise it seems like I'm the only one bringing something to the table."

Kai bounced his head up and down in a nervous action. "I hear you, man, and trust me I don't want to lose this deal. Listen, I've known you awhile now and I've been thinking that I could use another distributor for my own merchandise," Kai said with a twinge of nervousness.

Howard didn't readily answer. Instead, he met Kai's nervous stare and waited. "And?"

Kai looked in the direction of where Angeline was struggling to get in past the breaking waves. As she held onto her board for dear life, an idea formulated in his mind.

"I think I can even arrange something tonight," he said finally. "Hoagie, you're the man. You've got all these surfers and babes wanting your designs. I'll get you something else to sell them as well. And, who knows...maybe I can deliver the girl. Stay close to the phone."

"So, you're gonna give me a distribution deal? We're talking crystal meth?"

"The works. Meth, coke, even mephedrone and ketamine. And the girl!"

"Whatever, man. Girls are a dime a dozen. Just get me the goods." Howard gave him a high five and then swam toward the shore.

As Kai watched him leave, he whispered under his breath. "Just one big wipeout, little lady. That's all I need to play the hero that you will have no choice but to repay."

# # #

Chapter Twenty

One low life drug dealer on his beach was bad enough. The last thing Sam needed was to deal with a new guy as well. Addicts and their dealers were like sand fleas on a dog. You allow one to jump on board and the others follow suit. The only way to keep the beach clean was to rid it of the problem as soon as it surfaced and that was just what Sam intended to do.

"Can you take the watch?" Sam asked. "I'm going to see what this guy is up to," he motioned toward Howard who was walking to the parking lot with his surfboard in tow.

Evan nodded his agreement and took the binoculars from Sam. "You tell him, Sam."

Sam took off at a jog and easily caught up to Howard. "Hey, piece of advice for you. Your friend is bad news and he's going to go down. I'm going to make sure of it. If you know what's good for you, steer clear of him."

"That's unsolicited advice," Howard responded.

But as he turned away, Sam grabbed his elbow. "I'm not asking. I'm telling you." Sam may have started his time as a lifeguard begrudgingly, but it had turned into more than an assignment that brought him close to Angeline. He wasn't about to let this pristine beach become tainted. He knew how short life was and the good people who frequented this beach deserved a bit of happiness and beauty during their time on earth.

"Let's just relax," Howard said in a surprisingly calm tone. "I have no intention of causing any trouble." He spoke in an almost eloquent manner, one that was completely different to Kai's surfer speak.

Sam looked him up and down with a befuddled expression, not quite believing that the guy wasn't going to try something. "Listen, I don't have a reason to accuse you of any wrong doing, but I've got my suspicions about your friend, and one does judge people by the company they keep. Why don't you avoid him and we won't have a problem."

"Just because I'm associating with him doesn't mean we have a problem."

Sam crossed his arms and sighed with annoyance. This wasn't an easy conversation. He couldn't just accuse someone of being a drug user, but he had seen enough shady details surrounding Kai to instinctively know that the guy attracted bad news. "Kai is going to make a mistake and when he does, he'll pull everyone around him down with him. Why would you want to bring that unpleasantness on yourself?"

"Does that include the girl you have your eye on?" Howard gave him a pointed look, indicating that Sam wasn't the only one on the beach who paid attention to the daily happenings.

Sam narrowed his eyes. He was not going to let this guy get inside his head. Angeline was none of his business. "My job is to keep an eye on things here. That includes you. I'm trying to give you some friendly advice before you find yourself in trouble."

"I appreciate it." He turned to walk away, but once again, Sam stopped him, this time putting a firm hand on his shoulder, showing that he wasn't taking the situation lightly.

"Hey, are you going to steer clear of him or what?"

"I can't do that, man."

"Well, why the hell not?"

Howard shook his head and let his eyes look skyward as if waiting for an answer from above. "Let's just say that we want the same things. Maybe you should be the one to steer clear."

Sam placed his hands on his hips. This guy was really too much. He had a good mind to haul him out of here right on his... "You're something, you know that? Let me spell this out. Kai is a loser drug dealer. I know it. And if you're hanging out with him, then you know it too. Do I need to get the police out here?"

"I haven't broken any laws. Just remember that." Howard turned and walked to his car with quick strides. He was right of course. Sam didn't have anything concrete on either one of them, but at least he had made his point.

# # #

Chapter Twenty-One

Sam left the parking lot and returned to his lifeguard tower half expecting to find Angeline there, but when Evan told him that she was still in the water, he began to fume.

"That guy is an idiot! When is he going to bring her in?"

"All you can do is be here in case she needs you. Here." Evan handed him the binoculars that Sam had only put down moments earlier. "Keep a close eye."

Something in Evan's voice warned Sam that Angeline was in danger. Evan was a more experienced angel and had proven to have superior skills with regards to foreseeing danger. "You sense something?"

Evan nodded his head gravely. "Something's coming soon."

It happened in a split second. One minute Angeline didn't look like such a novice. She was actually enjoying a pretty good ride, but in the next her board flipped up from underneath her, flying high above and then to Sam's horror, it came crashing down, hitting her in the head. Angeline went under immediately.

Kai didn't seem to notice or if he did, he was too intent on his own ride to bother stopping for her. Sam and Evan both ran to the area, buoys and boards in hand as onlookers cleared a path. Their strides grew longer and faster until they hit the water at full speed.

Initially, their only mission was to locate Angeline who was still underwater, but the task at hand became more grave when Kai also went under, struck by an equally powerful wave.

"We're splitting up. You get him; I'll find Angeline," Evan barked the order.

Sam didn't like the assignment, but he had no choice. Besides, Kai was within reaching distance. When Kai's head emerged once more, Sam screamed at him. "Where is she? How could you keep her out here with waves like this?"

Kai's only response was to cough up the water that he was still taking in as one wave after another continued to pummel him. His arms flailed and panic started to set in, but Sam remained stony to his plight, holding him around the waist to prevent him from drowning but still indifferent to how close Kai came to losing his life.

"This is your fault," he said between gritted teeth, throwing Kai onto the rescue board.

"You're losing it out here," Evan said firmly from where he was treading water a few feet away. "You took an oath. You rescue people in need...that goes for him too."

Sam begrudgingly nodded his head and gave more support to a barely conscious Kai, holding him on the board while Evan continued to dive under looking for

Angeline. He was beginning to lose his faith when he saw her.

"Evan! There!" Sam pointed to just beyond where Evan floated. Immediately his co-worker dove for her. Sam saw a flash of lime green and knew that he had Angeline in his sights. He prayed with all his might and will to the God he served that she would be alright.

# # #

Chapter Twenty-Two

"I've got her," Evan said while hauling Angeline onto his board. Kai had come to and Sam didn't waste any time in giving him a few choice words.

"If I hadn't taken an oath to save people, I would so enjoy punching you out. I swear to God and believe me, I've got a direct line," he fumed to a bewildered Kai, "if you ever pull a stunt like that again."

"Sam, leave him," Evan said as they got to shore, and Sam didn't have to be told twice to help Evan transport the board carrying Angeline to the lifeguard tower.

Evan had administered CPR while still in the water, and although her heart was beating strongly, she was obviously suffering shock. Her eyes remained closed and a blue tinge traced her normally rouge lips. Bringing his ear to her heart, Sam had to be sure that she was alright.

"She just needs to get warm," Evan reassured him, while keeping an eye on Kai who had made his own way to the tower and was now huddled below it, wrapped in a towel that Evan had thrown his way. Sam gave him another cold stare to which Kai sheepishly looked away.

Sam was wrapping a blanket around Angeline, but signaled for Evan to come closer. "There has to be something...anything we can use to call in the police," he whispered. "I don't ever want to see him on this beach again."

Evan nodded. "I know, buddy, but you gotta play by the rules. We've got nothing. Yet."

Sam's normally clear, green eyes took on a cloudy tone when he saw Kai sauntering away, headed to the parking lot. The surfer still showed signs of being tossed around, but he wasn't nearly as bad off as Angeline and that made Sam even angrier.

"Evan, can you stay with Angeline until she's a bit stronger and ready to leave?"

"You know I will."

Sam nodded and yelled after Kai. "Hey, I want to talk to you." But the surfer merely flipped him off and kept on walking.

# # #

Chapter Twenty-Three

When Sam reached the parking lot, he saw that Howard was still there and was now speaking with Kai. Mumbling under his breath, he headed in their direction. "You two low lifes are not going to get away with this."

"We're in the middle of something." Howard said to Sam when he approached.

"You're joking, right?" Sam answered back.

Howard didn't seem to register that Sam had a look that said he wanted to punch his lights out. He just uttered another phrase designed to get Sam to leave. "I'll handle it from here. We're good."

Sam wasn't even close to being in the mood to deal with these two yahoos. "Good? I'll tell you when we're good. When you two never step foot on this beach again."

But Howard ignored him and instead took a step toward Kai, his back now turned toward Sam. Before Sam could object, he started speaking to Kai in phrasing that sounded an awful lot like he was reading Kai his Miranda rights.

"Kai Everett, you have the right to remain silent..."

"You're a narc?" Kai spoke up in what seemed like the first time since the accident.

"Anything you say or do can and will be used against you in a court of law...," Howard continued.

"This is so screwed up. I trusted you!"

Howard continued to ignore Kai's rants and continued speaking in his calm, professional voice. "You have the right to an attorney."

"You better believe I'm going to get an attorney. This is entrapment and total bullshit."

Howard finished his warning and looked up at Sam. "Sorry that I couldn't tell you. It wouldn't have worked if he suspected that I was anything other than what I pretended to be."

He cuffed Kai and led him to his car, where he opened the backseat, placed a hand on Kai's head to protect him, and directed him inside.

Once the door was shut and Kai was out of earshot, Sam extended his hand. "This is...wow, I'm really blown away. I'm sorry for giving you a hard time."

The two men shook hands and then Howard reached into his pocket to retrieve a business card. "I hope you won't need me, but in case you ever do. You were just doing your job as well. You really care about her, don't you?"

Sam couldn't help but allow a smile to slip. "More than heaven itself." As if a worrying thought suddenly crossed his mind, his brow furrowed. "Hey, about what he said...will this stick? I mean, you did...things that made him think you were on his side."

Howard shook his head. "Not those sort of things. A narcotics officer, especially an undercover one like myself, can never partake in the drugs, even if we're trying to establish ourself with a dealer, like Kai."

"But I thought..."

"So did he." Howard patted Sam on the back. "I'd bring him a sampling of drugs...just enough to show him that I could get the goods. He was so high after doing it that he never noticed that I was merely along for the ride. If I had broken protocol by partaking alongside him, that would surely result in a dismissal of the case and trust me, I've been on this one far too long to let that happen."

"How long are we talking?"

"Going on fifteen months. We could have gotten him much earlier on possession charges, but the bureau wanted more. He's a ringleader. He's got people under him and we needed to know when he pulled them in. I finally became his latest recruit...today. That was the break I needed."

"You didn't have anything else that would stick?" Sam's voice was ripe with worry. He didn't want to risk Angeline ever crossing paths with Kai again.

"Sure, I had plenty, but like I said, I was working on this case for over a year. Long term cases are the easiest for defense attorneys to attack because they try to imply that memories can be faulty."

Sam saw that Evan was returning with Angeline, a bandage now plastered on her forehead. He cringed with the memory of seeing harm come to her, but then caught himself and threw on a smile for her benefit.

"I want that guy put away. Tell me honestly. Do you have enough on him?"

Howard nodded, his expression serious. "Today was rough on your girlfriend..."

"She's not...well, I'd like her to be, but..."

Howard smiled. "I know what you mean. Anyway, I'm sorry she got mixed up in this. A few times I did my best to get her away from him. I didn't realize she wasn't the surfer he made her out to be. She'll be okay?"

"Yeah, she's pretty strong. My partner helped out in the water."

Howard nodded, obviously feeling poorly about a civilian getting hurt. "I have to say that if it wasn't for your girlfriend..." his voice trailed off and this time Sam just listened, not bothering to correct him. "Let's just say she made Kai get greedy and careless. Drug dealing is relatively small potatoes, but drug conspiracy is a whole different story."

Sam looked intrigued. "How so?"

"The first thing the prosecution needs for a conviction is evidence that a conspiracy existed. But the real clincher is if the defendant knowingly tried to further that conspiracy. That's what Kai did when he tried to recruit me. The case is a strong one."

"Would you say it's iron-clad strong?"

Howard rolled his head from side to side, not a move that gave Sam ultimate confidence. "I'm missing one thing," he admitted. "Kai's always been careful about leaving a trace. He only brings what he consumes so I've never had any extras to pocket."

At that moment, Evan approached with his arm around Angeline to guide her. Sam went to her immediately. "You okay?"

"Yeah...I think so. What's...why is he..."

"I'll explain it later." Sam kissed her forehead and helped her toward his car, then turned once more toward Howard and gave a small wave.

"Don't worry, Sam. Like I said, I wouldn't have opened up if I didn't feel it was time to prosecute. Have a good night and put all this out of your mind."

Sam opened the passenger door of his car to Angeline and watched as Howard got into his own car and drove Kai away from his beach...hopefully for good.

# # #

Chapter Twenty-Four

Sam turned to Angeline and patted the blanket around her like a mother hen. "You okay? Warm enough?"

Now considerably more alert, Angeline put her hand on Sam's arm. "Sam, I have to tell you something." Her voice was nothing more than a soft croak.

"Shhh, don't try and talk. Your throat is going to be sore from all of the salt water. Don't worry. I'll take care of you. I'm going to take you home."

"But...you must know..." she tried again.

"Later. I know you're probably upset and confused and I'm going to answer all of your questions, but you have to take care of yourself right now and that means resting your voice. I promise as soon as we get you home, I'll make you a hot drink and then we can talk."

Angeline shook her head vehemently. Sam could see how agitated she was and in spite of the obvious pain, she released a small whisper. "I need..." Her hand went to her throat and she closed her eyes, the pain being too great from just those few words.

Sam held her hand and brushed the hair off her face. Unable to help himself, he kissed her cheek. "I can't stand to see you hurt. Please, don't talk yet."

She nodded and looked in the back seat to where Sam had placed her beach bag. She pointed and Sam handed it to her, his eyes showing concern. She fumbled around in the bag and then produced a small, plastic bag. Its contents made Sam stare at her in disbelief.

Unable to stop himself he asked, "What is that?" in reference to the needle that was inside.

"Kai." She didn't need to say anything else. It was all Sam needed to clean up his beach. He pulled out his cell phone and immediately dialed the number on Howard's business card.

# # #

"I'm so stupid," Angeline sobbed. She had soaked in a hot bath that Sam had drawn for her, but her mood still hadn't warmed.

"How can you say that? It was an accident. That's all."

"An accident that could have been prevented if I hadn't been so stubborn." Angeline sat on the couch and looked over to where Sam was making dinner preparations in the kitchen.

He leaned his hands on the bar that separated the kitchen from the living room. "But Howard is going to make sure that Kai goes down for everything he's done. And you helped with that."

"I still feel like an idiot."

Sam joined her and handed her the cup of tea that she had placed on the coffee table in front of her. "Listen, what you call stubborn, I call brave. If most people were told they needed to start surfing in order to launch a clothing line, they would have backed down, but you not only accepted the challenge, you totally rocked it. You've learned a lot and look damn good out there."

She smiled as she did whenever Sam was around. His easy going nature and the way he looked at her always made her feel better. "Thank you for saying that. But still, I think I let my ego get in the way of common sense. And I'm sorry for how I treated you. I just didn't want anyone to tell me that I couldn't do it. I didn't really want to make you jealous and I never wanted him."

She stopped speaking and lowered her head, her eyes cast downward, unable to look Sam in the face. "I just thought Kai could help me break into designing. I didn't want to believe that he only wanted one thing."

When Angeline's emotions got the best of her and she had buried her head in her hands, Sam pulled her in close. Her back rested against his chest and he wrapped his arms around her. "You can't say anything that's going to change the way I feel about you."

"Kai was high. He was such a fraud. He even wanted to sell me off into a threesome. Well, he thought that's what was happening. I guess it was just part of Howard's game."

Sam held her even tighter as if he couldn't bear the idea of anyone hurting her.

"Kai thought I couldn't hear him when he was telling Howard how he would...never mind. It was right before..."

"Don't. You don't have to relive that. It's over."

Angeline nodded, a sad look crossing her features. "Sam?"

"Yes?" Sam turned her around to face him. "Hey, what's wrong?"

"You know that I never did anything with Kai. I kissed him once and afterward he proved to be the ass that he is. Nothing ever really happened. I need you to know that."

"I know that. I believe you." He kissed her forehead and closed his eyes, inhaling the scent of her lavender bath soap.

Angeline spoke softly, not wanting to break contact with Sam, but still needing to get the words out. "I feel as if my designs didn't have enough merit on their own."

"That's not true and I can prove it to you." Sam was now smiling widely.

For the first time since they had gotten home, Angeline seemed relaxed. She took in his playful nature and her eyes opened wide. "What aren't you telling me?"

"When you were upstairs Evan texted me to ask how you were. He told me that the mock-up of your ad fell out of your bag. When the crowd gathered round the lifeguard tower to find out what had happened to you, there were over twenty girls in line to find out where they could buy the bikinis in your portfolio."

"My look book? Are you serious?!" she said leaning forward and wrapping her arms around Sam's neck. "Oh my god, that's the best news ever. I don't need the Kai's of the world. I can get them made myself and sell them online."

"Apparently those girls all left their emails. They sent their best wishes to you and want you to add them to your mailing list as soon as you recover."

Angeline buried her head in the crook of Sam's neck between his jaw and shoulder. "Thank you. You are an angel."

"And you're mine," he replied softly, barely able to breathe due to the close proximity of her mouth. Their lips were practically touching and if he just lowered his head, even an inch. But he couldn't go there again. He shouldn't.

Chapter Twenty-Five

As if reading his thoughts, Angeline turned her head upwards. Her nose grazed his. Her mouth was close enough to kiss. He could feel her breath.

He didn't stand a chance. In fact, he hadn't from the moment he met her. He placed his fingers under her chin and tilted her face upwards so he could stare deeply into her beautiful green eyes.

During his time as an angel on earth, his love for Angeline had kept him from being with any other woman. But his lack of intimate relationships did not mean that he didn't possess other-worldly skills of seduction. One kiss from an angel makes every other experience pale in comparison and he wanted to show her this truth.

He loved her. Plain and simple. He understood the rules of guardian angels and knew they were partly designed to protect angels from falling for their assignments. But it was too late to save his heart. He didn't have to tell her, but he could show her how he felt. Cradling Angeline in his arms, he pulled her closer and pressed his mouth against hers with a kiss so passionate that it felt as if all the oxygen had left the room and they were breathless with their passion for each other.

# # #

They held each other on the couch and with each kiss Sam's resolve weakened just a bit more. When the night air brought a chill upon the room, Angeline shivered and moved even closer against him making him aware of every curve of her body.

Their dinner had been consumed, but the hunger within each of them was all consuming. And when Angeline innocently pointed upstairs, Sam lost his voice and any ability to argue. Holding hands, they slowly took to the stairs and when they found their way to Angeline's room, he reached his hand against the wall in search of the light switch, but Angeline promptly grabbed it, bringing it to her mouth and kissing the back of his hand.

"Are you sure you want me to stay?" Sam asked.

"Are you trying to make a quick get-away?" she teased.

"Never."

He meant it. With every fiber of his being, he wanted to stay with her forever. There would be no sleep tricks tonight.

Angeline moved easily in the dark, accustomed to her space. She reached inside a drawer and seconds later Sam heard the hiss of a match and then his eyes adjusted to the soft, flickering light of a candle she had lit.

He pulled his shirt over his head and she appraised his tanned and toned chest with approval. She followed suit, removing her robe and revealing that she wore only a thin babydoll nightie underneath.

Sam sucked in his breath, taking in her beauty. Once again, guilt started to plague his thoughts and he repeated his concern. "You're sure about this?" He reached for her hand and together they fell in the midst of her bed, the billowing comforter sinking below them.

"Very sure."

He asked twice and in his mind that had to account for something. He pulled down his jeans, then his underwear. When he revealed himself to her their flirty banter stopped. She eyed his masculinity with amazement as he was endowed like no man she had ever been with. When her momentary surprise washed away, she responded by taking his member in her hands and bringing her mouth down over him. She ran her tongue over the length of him and sucked the head, all the while using her hand to slide up and down his enormous shaft.

Sam closed his eyes and leaned back against the pillows of her bed. The idea of stopping her could not be retrieved from the depths of his mind. He could think of nothing except her beautiful mouth making love to his thankful rod. As she sucked him closer to climax, he recovered his strength of will. When he pulled back he wasn't stopping her for the sake of maintaining his vows, but rather to show her what angels were capable of.

# # #

He lifted the nightie over her head and gently rolled her onto her back. As he leaned down to kiss her neck, his leg inched hers over, bringing their naked bodies upon each other.

If she changed her mind right then and pulled away, he wouldn't have argued. He would have reasoned that it was for the best. But she didn't. Instead, she arched her back and pressed her chest against his, offering up her mouth to him which he kissed, hard. She opened her mouth and his tongue wound around hers.

He could have kissed her until the end of time and been satisfied in doing just that, but she reached down under the covers, running her hand between his thighs until she held him tightly. He moaned, but stopped her. "Your turn," he said with a determined tone. "Lie back."

She did as he asked, staring up at him, mesmerized at the ethereal quality of his demeanor. She felt total comfort in his presence as if he would love her until the end of time. And as if to demonstrate this, he bent his head and kissed her body with a fervor that had built up over the last few weeks. He didn't just kiss her, he savored her, moving his mouth from hers, down every inch of her body until he stopped just above her pubic bone.

He slowly moved his tongue over the mound of her, settling himself between her legs. When she whimpered and begged for him to kiss her there, he obliged the request, diving his tongue between the folds of her lips and tasting her sweetness.

"Oh please, Sam. Don't stop. Not this time."

# # #

Chapter Twenty-Six

She didn't need to voice this because he couldn't imagine anything so wonderful as giving her pleasure. He reached his hands under her hips and pulled her deeper toward him, taking her to a place that rocked her core as his tongue continued to flutter over her.

"I want you inside of me."

"I need to be there," he answered and lifted himself onto her. A moan escaped her mouth as he entered her and Sam muffled the sound with his own mouth. Their kiss intensified as their movements became one. The heat they generated left each one breathless and soon they had no choice but to stop their kiss and focus on the wonderful ride as their hips rose and fell against each other, moving themselves to a height that felt like heaven itself.

"Slow down, Angel," he whispered.

He knew this might be the last time he would be with her, so he poured his soul into that very moment.

"I don't want to."

"Oh hell."

He rolled them over so that she was now on top of him and with her legs straddled on either side of his body, he easily slid in and out. Being one with her was a heaven he had never known. His head was dizzy with the overwhelming emotions he felt for her and given the words she whispered, he knew she felt it too.

"It's so soon that I can't believe I'm saying this, but I think I'm falling for you."

"I feel the same way," Sam told her and placed his hands on her hips and slowly thrust into her. Her hands balanced on his chest and he gazed into her eyes before their movements made her throw her head back and a sound of pure enjoyment escaped her mouth. Sam watched her beautiful body and reached up to cup each of her breasts.

"I don't want this to end; you feel so good."

He closed his eyes, feeling her body clench around him. His hands found her hips and moved her in time with his thrusts, relishing the way her body responded as they approached climax.

Only when he felt her spasm around him did he allow himself a release. She wrapped her legs tightly around his waist and rode the wave that carried both of them through their orgasm. Their hands searched each other frantically, both caught in their need and love for each other.

Afterwards, she lay in his arms and expressed her feelings more definitively. "I am in love with you." She fell asleep before he could even tell her the same.

# # #

Chapter Twenty-Seven

The sun streamed through the window and the early morning brought with it the sound of birds chirping. With Angeline still nestled in Sam's arms, it was an idyllic way to wake, but worry filled his mind.

He lay staring at the ceiling, waiting for something to happen. For her to wake up and look at him with an expression of regret. Or for a long lost boyfriend to pound on the front door. He knew that he wasn't supposed to be with her and this felt too perfect. Something had to happen.

But when Angeline awoke, she turned to Sam with the most beautiful smile, a look of such warmth it could thaw the coldest winter day.

"Good morning," he said sunnily.

She nuzzled his neck and kissed his cheek. Sam immediately felt his reaction as did she when she pressed against him. "It is a good morning," she replied lustily and climbed on top of him.

They kissed passionately and Sam wished for a repeat of the previous night, but part of him didn't dare push his luck. He beat the odds. He got the girl. But he had made a promise to God and he knew the consequences could be grave if he broke it.

Just as his thoughts turned to fear, ironically Angeline's did as well. Propping herself up on an elbow, she turned toward Sam. "Want to hear something crazy?"

"That sounds like a loaded question."

She affectionately threw a pillow at his head. "I'm serious."

"Tell me. You can't say anything crazy."

She took a deep breath, her nerves suddenly blooming with what she planned to say. Finally, she spoke in a small voice. "When I was being tossed around by those waves, I never feared losing my life. The only thing that scared me was the thought of not seeing you again."

Sam got a nervous twinge in his stomach and in spite of himself, he let his eyes drift toward the ceiling and away from Angeline.

"Sam? I guess that doesn't make sense. I mean, the only way we wouldn't see each other would be if something horrible happened. Right?"

Sam swallowed hard. He wanted to tell her that there wasn't even a remote chance that their relationship wouldn't continue. But he knew the risk of saying such a thing. She stared at him, waiting. As seconds approached a minute, a tear fell down the side of her cheek and it tore him up.

He couldn't hurt her. He wouldn't. He reasoned that he wasn't that kind of man when he was a human and he wouldn't be that kind of man when cloaked as an angel.

"Angeline...that day when the waves were big and you were scared...you remember?

She nodded.

"I told you then...you're safe with me."

Her tear stained face brightened instantly with the knowledge that Sam cared just as deeply about her. She threw her arms around Sam's neck and fortunately, couldn't see the worry on his face.

As they both settled back onto the pillows, an idea formed in Sam's mind. Marriage.

God would never deliberately part two people joined in marriage. What he wouldn't give to spend the rest of his life with Angeline. They would hold a ceremony joining them in matrimony, before a congregation in a house of worship. In God's eyes that would have to account for something.

He recalled one particular line of a traditional wedding vow: *What God has joined together, let no one separate.* He felt strongly that this would allow him to remain with Angeline without breaking the rules of angels.

He took her hand in his own. "Angeline, I want you to marry me."

"What?" Angeline's face registered with surprised, but then she threw back the covers and stood up on the mattress doing a little happy dance of excitement. Sam immediately jumped up and took her hands in his own. The two bounced on the mattress and laughed like children before finally settling back down onto the bed.

Angeline turned toward him. "You're serious, right? Because that's not the kind of thing you say to a girl who loves you...unless you love her right back."

"I love you right back and I want you to marry me." He leaned into her and held Angeline in a firm embrace, bringing their lips together.

"We should celebrate," she announced with giddy excitement.

"I know just the thing to start off our day. You stay right here because I want to jump right back in bed with you as soon as I return."

"Where are you going?"

"To bring back coffees and scones, of course." He gave her one more kiss, this time on the cheek, and when he stood, she blew him another.

Sam retrieved his cell phone from the bedside table and unlocked the touch screen. "Hey, do that again. Blow me a kiss."

He aimed his phone at her and the sound of the camera shutter went off. "Now I can see you even when I'm in line."

"Well, I don't have a photograph so don't make me wait too long."

# # #

Chapter Twenty-Eight

"Listen, Sam's a good egg. A lousy angel, perhaps, but a good soul. I'm sure there's a reasonable explanation." Evan pleaded his friend's case to God, who looked at the screen showing Sam kiss Angeline before leaving her home a few minutes prior.

"Evan, I appreciate your loyalty, but I am all seeing and all knowing. He wasn't exactly forced into this relationship."

"But certainly you can see that it's a byproduct of his dedication to the job?" Evan knew the minute he let the thought escape his mouth that it would be met by skepticism and indeed, God raised his eyebrows with a look of disbelief.

"Choices. We are all faced with them."

"So does this mean?" Evan tried to get to the crux of the matter.

"Evan...do you believe me to be fair?"

"Of course I do, it's just that...well, you know. Sam's young, a bit impetuous, but he does mean well. He made a mistake. But, don't we all?" Evan wore a worried expression for his friend.

"You're going to have to trust me on this one. Send him in, please."

# # #

Sam rounded the corner from Angeline's place and headed onto San Vicente Boulevard. The tree lined center divider doubled as a shady refuge for joggers and Sam decided to join them. He put his earbuds in place and sang along to Adam Levine, feeling happier than he could ever imagine.

"Sugar...you're sweet," he sang, thinking of Angeline. He ran a bit faster, not wanting to waste a minute away from her, and knowing that it was imperative that they start their wedding plans as soon as possible.

The coffee shop was up ahead and he sighed seeing that the line was painfully long. He looked around quickly to see if there was another place he could pick up pastries and coffee. The music in his ears reached the chorus and Sam felt like he was on Cloud Nine. He was just giving thought to where the humans came up with that little phrase when Adam Levine hit his falsetto and Sam raised his voice right along with him. He didn't even hear the high pitch squeal of tires barreling down on him as he made a sudden decision to cross the street in favor of a different shop.

# # #

The impact was quick and swift.

"Sam? Are you okay?"

Sam felt shaken and gazed up at the sky from his vantage point. He rested on his back in the midst of the once busy street where the traffic had come to a standstill and sirens could be heard approaching from a distance.

The voice spoke again to him. "Sam? Can you hear me?"

"Evan? What are you doing here?"

He didn't mince words. "You're time as an angel is being reevaluated. I've come to take you back."

That was enough to get Sam moving. He sat up, although the form that was his body remained still. "What do you mean? Listen, I don't want to know. Just...just give me some time to explain things to Angeline."

"You can't explain anything in that body." Evan winced, trying not to draw attention to Sam's condition. "But don't worry, they'll issue you a new body."

"What do you mean?"

"Sam, you can't pretend that you don't know what's happening. You know the rules. They can't be ignored."

Sam shook his head vehemently. "No. No! I'm not hearing this from you. You're supposed to be my friend. This isn't up to you. I want to see God. I'm sure we can settle this. My situation with Angeline has changed."

But Evan simply shook his head, looking pained at his friend's stubborn refusal to see things for what they were. "Sam, we need to go. Speak to him in person."

After a moment, the fight left him and reality set in. Sam nodded his head solemnly. Then, he pulled his phone from his back pocket. The screen was cracked, but he gave a sigh of relief when it came to life with the touch of his thumbprint. He opened the camera roll and stared at the photo of Angeline he had taken just that morning.

"Sam? What are you doing?"

"I need to remember her. I have to memorize her beautiful face. Just in case."

# # #

Chapter Twenty-Nine

The journey was never easy, but Sam reminded himself that seldom is something one finds to be worthwhile. At the very least he could take comfort in knowing he had cleaned up his beach. But no sooner had his thoughts focused on the beach when they turned to Angeline, her pure nature, her beautiful smile, those bikinis, and then, he found himself staring into the face of God.

"Shit."

"I beg your pardon?"

"I'm sorry. I didn't mean any disrespect. It's just that...oops, I did it again."

God raised his eyebrows at Sam's attempt at humor. An awkward pause ensued and Sam explained himself. "I was singing at the time of the accident. Not Britney Spears, mind you, but I wasn't really paying attention the way I should have been."

He looked down at himself and what appeared to be his unharmed body. He exhaled in relief. "Thanks for saving my butt...err, me...thanks for saving me, God."

"Please don't break into a rendition of *Amazing Grace*."

"No, I wouldn't think of it. I wasn't even planning it," Sam reassured him.

"Good. Because the truth is you've really done a number on your body. Again."

God looked down at his notes as Sam waited in silence with the exception of the occasional rumble of his stomach. "Sorry, I was on my way to get breakfast."

"I know, Sam. I know about everything."

Sam swallowed and licked his lips. Everything. That was a pretty lofty word. He suddenly wondered just how much eavesdropping God actually did. "When you say 'everything' does that mean you know the generalities or the specifics?"

"I don't need to watch everything to get an understanding of what's going on. I'm referring to your relationship with Angeline being more than platonic and extending far beyond the boundaries of the guardian angel rules."

"I'm sorry. I truly am sincere when I say that." Sam shuffled nervously. He realized at that moment just how serious this could get.

"Sam, I know you're sorry and to a degree I understand that you were placed in a difficult situation. Your assignment bonded with you and you are a kind soul who felt obliged to offer comfort. I can see where one might get carried away."

"Oh that's a relief," Sam interjected. "For a minute I thought I was really in trouble."

God looked at him sternly and didn't readily answer.

"I'm not in trouble, am I? Sir?"

"You were a good guardian angel to her, Sam, but that doesn't excuse you. This isn't a mistake you can take back. You can't change her destiny."

"But I think I am her destiny. We're going to get married."

God raised his eyebrows.

"It's true," Sam insisted. "And you'll be there, so to speak. We'll take new vows and it will be forever. I can't leave her, God."

"Sam, don't make this more difficult than it already is. I am a just God, but there are rules."

"Please. Please don't send me away from her." The distraught look on Sam's face was immeasurable. "I'm not asking for myself, God. She's expecting me back and I just can't bear to think of her waiting on me after what just transpired. She'll think I abandoned her." Then, in a voice not much above a whisper, he added, "She loves me."

When God didn't answer, Sam's thoughts went into overdrive.

"Oh no," he said with sudden realization. "She'll find out that I got hit by that car. No! She'll blame herself. I know she will. She'll think if only she didn't agree to the chocolate chip scone! Please, it's bad enough that half the population has given up carbs, don't give her a reason to jump on that bandwagon."

"I'm not unreasonable, Sam. And I don't want you to think that you're being punished. That's not how it works."

"It does sort of feel that way."

A plush velvet, wing-backed chair slid forward. "Please, take a seat. Would you like a cup of tea?"

Sam nodded. "Cream and sugar, please."

"Of course. Hungry?"

"Yes, actually."

God typed something onto an ipad that dropped from the ceiling and seconds later, a full breakfast was wheeled in by two small cherubs. After Sam took a few bites of his sausage and eggs, he appeared more relaxed.

"Very good. Now, let me continue," God said. "We often hear humans talk about living in the moment. That is an excellent proposition, but one still must behave responsibly. You were a good angel, Sam. There's no doubt that you maintained a careful watch over Angeline. You obviously cared for her...perhaps too much. There is a certain amount of autonomy in the work of an angel, but the rules are there to protect angels and humans alike."

"But why?" Sam pleaded. "I took care of her. I will always take care of her."

"We are not the same species, Sam. It's really that simple."

Sam was less agitated now that he had eaten. He spoke softly and deliberately. "I don't know if I could do anything differently," he admitted. "When you love someone as strongly as I did...as I do, it's hard to walk away."

"I understand the dilemma you faced. But that's where free will and choice comes in. Please stand."

Sam stood up, knowing that his fate rested with what God would say and do next.

"Again, choices. You can go back to Earth as a human. You may rest assured that you have fulfilled your duties as an angel and you may be returned. But, you won't have any memory of your work as an angel."

Sam appeared confused. "What does that mean? What about Angeline?"

"You won't remember having met her either. And, she won't remember you. Basically, the last three months will be wiped away."

"And if I remain an angel?"

"You'll be reassigned and you still won't remember Angeline." God picked up a telephone and spoke into it. "Send in Evan, please."

"What does Evan have to do with this?" Sam asked.

Evan walked into the room and took the seat next to Sam. "How are you doing, buddy?"

"Eh, been better," Sam admitted.

"At least you didn't mess up your face this time. That's something?" Evan offered.

"True."

"Gentlemen Angels, may I continue?"

"Please," Sam and Evan answered together.

"Thank you. If you decide to remain a guardian angel, Evan will still be asked to take over your current assignment. We don't want the same mistakes happening again. Evan is familiar with her case and won't fall prey to the same temptations."

Sam looked to Evan, who just shrugged his shoulders. "Sorry, mate."

"Perfect. Either way I lose the girl."

"Nobody said life was easy. But I've heard that a life worth living is one worth fighting for." Evan gave him a look of encouragement.

Sam thought about his friend's words and God's choices. "So you think I should do it? I should go back as a human?"

"You'll be human. You can find love. If your time as an angel is any indication of how you'll live the rest of your human life, I'd say that people on Earth would be lucky to call you a friend. Come here." Evan pulled Sam in for a hug. The two men patted each other on the back before stepping apart.

"It's been good working with you, Evan. I hope that someday I'll run into you and maybe you'll give me some of that famous advice of yours."

"You bet I will. You're going to be okay, Sam. Just have faith."

Sam turned toward God and nodded once that he was ready. With a clap of thunder, the clouds opened up and rain poured down. The winds blew and the sky turned from blue to gray and then back again. And when the storm had passed, a rainbow appeared over the horizon bringing awe to everyone who witnessed it.

# # #

Epilogue

The morning had been greeted by an unseasonal summer storm, but now that it had stopped Sam planned to hit the beach. He circled the block looking for a parking spot near his favorite coffee house, deciding to grab a cup before heading down the canyon. As he parked his car, he stared up at the sky, noticing a beautiful rainbow cresting over the Hollywood Hills. It appeared to be close enough that one could imagine being able to climb up its arch.

A pretty girl hurried past, but stopped as others did to admire the sight. Her golden hair and porcelain complexion caught his eye and he thought to himself that she was a sight more beautiful than even the rainbow. He gathered his wits and headed into the coffee house, pleased to see that she had taken the same course.

When they both arrived at the door simultaneously, Sam rushed in front of her to hold it open.

"Oh, thank you." Her voice had a lyrical quality to it. The voice of an angel, Sam thought to himself.

"My pleasure. After you."

"You sure? The line's long."

It wasn't hard for Sam to turn on the charm, not where this girl was concerned. She had a glow about her, something Sam might even call an aura. In short, there was something about her that drew him to her. "Something tells me if you keep me company the time will pass faster than I want it to."

She blushed and started to walk through the door as he held it, along with another man who hurried in right after her. "Oh hey man, thanks!" The guy carried more than a few extra pounds around his mid-section.

"No problem," Sam muttered and then took his place in line, now one person away from the girl of his dreams.

She turned to look over her shoulder and flashed him a smile, but the man in front of Sam mistook the gesture as meant for him. "You come here often?" he said, trying the oldest line in the book to strike up a conversation.

Sam rolled his eyes, but kept them planted firmly on her as she politely answered. "Every morning," she said cheerily and then to Sam's delight she met his gaze and continued, "I like the clientele here."

He smiled back at her, but his look turned to surprise and then concern as her heel slipped on a wet tile and she lost her balance. He moved immediately to catch her, but she landed in the arms of the guy standing directly behind her...the spot that Sam knew should have been his. *Lucky guy. He wasn't even trying. She just landed in his arms. Like a gift from above.*

And as the thought hit Sam's psyche, he decided to do something about it.

"Are you okay?" he asked with concern, stepping in front of her and helping her to her feet.

She hadn't yet answered, but Sam only took that as a sign of her surprise and perhaps embarrassment. "Here, allow me," he said to the man awkwardly holding the girl who looked like an angel. "Go ahead, you can take my place in front," Sam motioned to the barista waiting to take the next order.

"Thanks again, man," he said and then awkwardly passed her over to Sam's waiting arms.

She smiled at the absurdity of the moment, but then laughed outright when Sam broke the ice yet again. "I'd say we have to stop meeting like this, but that would not only be a cliche, but also a lie. I'm Sam." He extended his hand to her and when she took it in her own, a shock hit both of them.

Rather than pull her hand away, she merely put the other one on top of Sam's. "This is an old trick. You can't get shocked if you form a hand sandwich."

"Is that true?" Sam asked with amusement.

"It's working, isn't it?"

Neither one made any attempt to remove their hands. The mood between them shifted and the joking was replaced by seriousness as they took in each other's expressions. "I'm Angeline."

"It's a pleasure to meet you."

They had moved aside so the line could pass, but they continued to stare intensely at each other.

"I know this sounds crazy, but I'm about to go surfing and I'd love some company."

Angeline stared at him in earnest. "I don't know...I'm a bit accident prone to tell you the truth. Me and surfing? That's probably a bad idea."

"Come on, the only bad idea would be to say no."

It was a bold statement. Sam had never been so forward with a woman and for that matter, Angeline would never normally entertain such a thought, but she found herself wanting to talk to him a bit longer.

"Have your coffee with me. If I haven't convinced you by the time you finish, then you'll go home and I'll go to the beach. At least we won't be drinking our coffees alone."

Angeline nodded. "I guess I can't argue with that logic. Coffee is much more enjoyable when it's shared."

She followed Sam outside of the coffee house and they continued their conversation by one of the sidewalk tables. Suddenly the large set man who had taken Sam's place in line came barreling out of the coffee house. Sam instinctively put an arm around Angeline, pulling her in close to him.

The man stopped in his tracks before bumping into her, but nevertheless spilled scalding coffee in her direction. "Oh wow, I'm really sorry. Are you okay?" he asked while trying to sip up the coffee that was dripping over the side of his cup.

"We're good," Sam answered for the both of them and watched the guy continue on with his day.

Still in the safety of Sam's arms, Angeline looked up at him. "Thank you. He was certainly in a hurry."

"Yeah. It's funny, but I suddenly feel like time is standing still."

Sam couldn't help himself. He should have released his hold on her, but he felt like this was a girl he needed to keep close. "So, about surfing?"

"I don't know," she hesitated.

"You're safe with me."

Angeline looked at Sam as if seeing him in a different light. "What did you say?"

"It was nothing."

"No, it wasn't. When that guy knocked me over, you were there. And when he nearly spilled hot coffee on me..." Angeline touched the palm of her hand to Sam's cheek.

He smiled at her and asked, "Is that a yes?"

"Someone else used to say that to me. The part about being safe with you. It sounds weird, but I don't remember anything else, just that I believe you. I feel like I've met you before."

Sam took her hand and they walked up San Vicente Boulevard, dodging the joggers and the early morning walkers, the slow-paced window shoppers and the hurried workers. "Let's go to the beach."

"We should thank that guy," Angeline commented and Sam immediately knew who she meant.

"Yeah, I guess the angels were watching over us today."

# # #

If you enjoyed this book, please consider posting a review. Reviews are integral for indie authors to successfully promote themselves. I thank you in advance for your valuable time. It means the world to me.

About the Author

Mia Fox is a Los Angeles-based novelist who writes across varied genres including Contemporary and Paranormal Romance, Chick Lit, and Satire. She received her Bachelor of Arts Degree in Communications from U.S.C.

Before writing full time, she worked as an entertainment publicist, a career she chronicles in her novel, "Alert the Media." However, she is happy to leave that world behind her, preferring that any drama in her life is only that which she creates for her characters.

She lives in Los Angeles with her husband, three children, Casey, the Wonder Westie, and Bean, his brother.

Stay in touch with Mia...

You can stay in touch with me across various social media channels. Pick your favorite...or all of them!

http://miafox.net/

https://www.facebook.com/MiaFoxBooks

http://www.amazon.com/Mia-Fox/e/B00CXZQ84C

https://twitter.com/MiaFoxBooks

https://www.goodreads.com/author/show/7036109.Mia_Fox

https://instagram.com/MiaFoxBooks

https://booktropoloussocial.com/index.php?do=/profile-2507/

http://miafoxbooks.tumblr.com/

http://www.tsu.co/MiaFoxBooks

Also by Mia Fox...

Romani Realms Series
(paranormal romance)

Released (book one)
Resurrected (book two)
Returned (coming soon)

Chasing Shadows Series
(contemporary/paranormal romance)

Believe (book one)
Trust (book two)

Hollywood Hotties Series
(chick lit)

Alert the Media
Keeping Up

Surprise Passion Series
(humorous erotica)

Ready for the Yeti (book one)
Going Steady with the Yeti (book two)
Scent of the Centaur (book three)
Ethel and the Merman (book four)

Guardian Angel Series
(paranormal/contemporary romance)

Malibu Angel
and more to come!

www.ingramcontent.com/pod-product-compliance
Lightning Source LLC
Chambersburg PA
CBHW060055150626
46556CB00017BA/736